Lori and her best friend, Tulip are going horse-packing. They're heading away from civilisation and into the wilderness. There are ruined churches and lost villages to discover; deserted lochs to swim in and ancient forests to explore. They won't bother with tents and food, they'll build shelters and forage for their meals and they're looking forward to searching out wildlife; badgers, goats, deer, dragonflies, goshawks and maybe even wild cats or pine martens.

Although they'll avoid towns, villages and people as much as they can, the real world is never that far away ... and they'll never turn away if they think they can help.

BEYOND THE CROW POST

A J Anderson

Wire
Bridge
Books

For M

The start of the summer holidays

My full name is Lorelei Römer although everyone calls me Lori … everyone except Dad. Dad always, always uses my full name, he's like that, which is probably why he's an accountant. Anyway, pedantic Dad and I were having a bit of father-daughter time, reading an article on how to do cryptic crosswords. To be honest I'd always thought crosswords were boring, you either knew the answer or you didn't but actually it was more like there was a secret code and you could work out the solution even if you didn't know what the word at the end meant.

Mum came down the stairs; she'd been putting Fearghus, my little brother, to bed and she had that look that something was bugging her.

'What's up Mum?' I asked, 'someone made an oily mess with a bit of an old motor?'

Dad instantly denied it could be anything to do with him. 'Old car parts in the house, what a ridiculous idea.' He gave a nervous laugh.

'Are there?' she asked.

He shook his head and tried to look as innocent as possible.

'There'd better not be, I don't want any of those dirty, rusty things near our new carpets.'

'Is it Gus then, is he okay?' I asked.

'The boy … he's fine, it's that rubbish book he insisted I

read to him. I think it's called "Testing Times"? He said it's his favourite, is that right?'

Me or Dad are usually on reading duties.

'Is that the latest one from the Spy Boy series? They're brilliant, mum, they're so exciting,' I said. 'I'll have to grab it when he's finished.'

'But it's so unrealistic, just ridiculous!'

'They're great,' chipped in dad. 'Turbo-charged versions of the books I loved when I was growing up.'

'But the kids in them! … On page one they can hardly say boo to a goose, three pages later, their parents have been kidnapped and they're locked in the cellar. Turn over the next page and they've escaped, somewhat miraculously it must be said, and they start searching for their mum and dad. Everywhere they turn there's another ridiculous conspiracy or some over-muscled, scar-faced thug ready to tear them apart … but what do you know, they're experts in karate, can ride motorcycles and even skydive; skills that have never been mentioned before they're in a situation that needs them. If that's not preposterous enough, they soon make short shrift of a variety of increasingly unlikely villains and physical challenges. I mean they start off as puny, little, "Nervous Neddies" and for Christ's sake within days they're thrashing grown adults in hand-to-hand combat.'

'They're adventure stories,' pointed out Dad, 'they're not meant to be real. They're giving the readers a fantasy world they can daydream about and pretend it's them who're saving the world or whatever.'

'But it's such nonsense, kids need books that show them what the world is actually like.'

'That'd be a bit boring for an adventure novel,' I suggested, 'they'll probably be spending most of their adult lives in an office this is a chance to spark their imagination.'

Personally I think the spy boy books are brilliant, any sort of adventure story is okay with me. When I'm visiting my friends Ewan, Catriona and Angus, we pretend we live in the castle near them and we have to defend it from foreign invaders, or fierce monsters, or maybe the king is visiting and it's up to us to arrange a spectacular pageant. When Tulip and I are together, Tulip's my best friend, sometimes we make out we're tribesmen roaming the land, or when we're out on the horses we're cowboys or posh Victorian explorers collecting specimens or Cossacks living on the steppes keeping the borders safe and at school I'm the first to sign up to be in the plays.

'They're not remotely rooted in the real world,' complained Mum.

'The real world is even weirder,' I pointed out, 'what about Tulip, I mean she has some properly amazing skills and she's just my age?'

'That's a completely different kettle of fish, aside from that you're mainly just riding the horses and exploring like lot of other kids, you're not saving the world between lessons, which is what these kids are doing every second chapter!'

'Yes but ...'

'Unless you've been doing it in secret, I'm pretty sure you

and Tulip haven't been defusing missiles, piloting jet planes, rescuing Prime Ministers or assisting Nobel prize winning scientists with their preposterous inventions,' mum said.

'No but ...'

'But what?'

'I'm not meant to say but actually I've been recruited for a super top-secret job ...'

'Yes,' said Mum suspiciously.

'Yes,' I agreed. 'I've been put on the case of a sinister super-villain – the "Cake-taker"! I was drafted in by MI5 when that chocolate gateaux went missing, luckily the thief left some clues; oily fingerprints, the catalogue for a vintage car rally and a well-used calculator.'

'Probably not worth pursuing those leads,' suggested dad.

Mum just raised her eyebrows at him.

Mum and dad don't know everything about Tulip, just that she has some special talents. I've never told them the truth because they wouldn't believe it ... that's because ... she's a ... well she's not human ... she's a goblin! You can't tell to look at her, since she doesn't have pointy ears or anything weird. She's the same age as me, a little taller, her hair is wild as anything and she always wears lots of rings, brooches and silver jewellery. They think she travels about with her family so she can only stay with us when they're back in our area but actually she comes from a different place and can only cross over when there's a new moon. I've been back with her and someday I've going to try and describe what it's like there, because it's so different from here.

Tulip can do some properly weird things, one of the few things I have told Mum and Dad about is, that if someone is ill, she can tell. When Fearghus was a baby, she sensed he had a virus and said I had to make mum take him to the hospital; she saved his life. What they don't know is that if she's racing to go somewhere she can disappear and then reappear ten feet further on and they don't know that some plants really like her and they'll look after her if she needs help. I have some really best friends, but Tulip is more than a best friend, she's like a sister.

'Okay, we haven't been saving the world,' I conceded, 'but it is a little weird and a bit like the books Gus likes us to read to him.'

Mum reluctantly acknowledged it was different.

'I'm glad it's her turn to visit,' interrupted Dad. 'We miss you when you go off with her family.'

Because the barriers are only down on a new moon, when we go between our worlds we have to stay until the next new moon before we can come back, so when I go over, I'm there for a month.

'I miss you too, you know,' I said.

'That's very kind of you to say,' said Dad, 'and do you miss your Mum ...'

She didn't let him finish and gave him a playful punch on the arm. 'It's going to be lovely to see Tulip again,' she said.

I agreed, I was already getting excited as there were only a couple more sleeps 'til the next new moon and then Tulip would be here.

The planning

The next morning, I buzzed down to the farm to give them a hand. Mrs. Lindsay, the farmer's wife, is going to have a baby so she can't do all the things she normally does, so if I'm free I help out.

Once the chores were done, I popped in to say hello and check she was okay. I made us a pot of tea and we sat in the sun to chat.

'So, Lori, any plans for when Tulip comes to stay?' she asked.

I think Mrs. Lindsay knows about Tulip and where she really comes from. We've never talked about it, she's never asked me any questions and she's never said anything to Tulip but I'm pretty sure she's worked it out.

'Normal stuff for most of the time, but first we're going to head off somewhere remote, stay as far from people as we can and explore,' I said.

'A walking holiday?'

'Yeah,' I agreed, 'just the two of us. I've a rough plan and we'll see what we come across …'

'Could I ask a favour … perhaps instead of walking could you take Finn and Oliver?'

Finn and Oliver are her horses.

She explained how they weren't getting the exercise they need, 'it'd be good for them. To be honest they're getting lazy and bored mooching round the same fields every day.'

'Really? That would be so amazing!'

'You both like riding and you'd be able to go a lot further and quicker,' said Mrs. Lindsay.

'Are you sure?'

She nodded.

'I'd be super happy and Tulip would love it,' I conceded.

'I know you'll look after them but more importantly they'll look after you.'

'They will,' I agreed, 'people don't mess with you when you're on a horse.'

'They're big lumps,' pointed out Mrs. Lindsay.

Her horses are huge, and there's not much of either of us, we're skinny, little scraps mainly, but it's like they understand us. I think it's because we never use saddles so they can sense how we're feeling and sort of know the way we want to go or if we're getting ready for a jump almost before we do.

'If you're sure …' I said.

'Yes for sure. They really need to get away from the same fields, especially Oliver.'

'I was planning to be away for a week, is that okay? We could come back earlier.'

She said a week was fine and patted her tummy, 'it's not as if I'll be doing much riding … or even grooming while you're off.'

'If we're away for a few days we'll need stuff won't we, I mean for the horses?' I said.

'Hmm … let's look at the bare minimum,' she said. 'I suppose you two will have little more than what you're standing up in?'

I agreed, Tulip and I don't take much when we go wandering. We don't need food as we forage, we build shelters and we know how to navigate across the countryside; so basically it's just a change of knickers, a big t-shirt to wear when we're washing everything else, a waterproof each, our knives and a mobile phone for emergencies.

Mrs. Lindsay listed some of the things Finn and Oliver needed, 'food because they can't just eat grass, you'll need to groom them and check hooves so you'll need that kit and of course a saltlick.'

Once the list was done, we had a stroll to the stables to see what was already there and what I'd need to buy.

Finn saw me and called me over with a whinny.

'It's funny …' Mrs. Lindsay mused aloud.

'What is?' I asked.

'Finn is the more adventurous of the two of them,' she said, 'while Tulip is far more daring than you …'

'She might be a little more daring,' I didn't like admitting it out loud even if it was true.

'But Finn prefers to be with you and sensible old Oliver gets on better with Tulip.'

I rubbed Finn's flank and fed him a carrot. 'I'd never thought about it, but you're right,' I agreed. 'I wonder why, do you think it's opposites attracting?'

'Could be,' she said. After thinking about it she added, 'maybe Finn thinks you'll keep him right but if he and Tulip were together they might take too many risks?'

That's true. Tulip likes excitement and if there's any chance for a thrill, she'll go for it. I'm quite cautious, which actually is just as well or she'd have got herself into a ton more trouble.

Before we left, I went over to say hello to Sally so she didn't feel left out. Sally is Mrs Lindsay's first horse and I learnt to ride on her but she's getting on a bit so she gets to do her own thing now and take things easy.

Day 1
Chapter 1

The barriers between our worlds are weakest at midnight so I went to the secret garden at eleven, hung around outside until Tulip appeared and took her home. We hadn't seen each other for a month and we talked most of the night, which meant the following day was a bit of a washout. We spent the day pottering sleepily about the house, playing with Gus and doing stuff for mum.

The next morning, after we'd had a proper sleep, we headed to the farm just after sunrise. Mr. Lindsay was already at work.

'Hi Mr. Lindsay,' Tulip gave him a hug. 'I've totally missed you.'

'Morning Tulip, you've brought the good weather with you.'

He didn't bat an eye at the way we were dressed even though it was pretty eccentric. I love colour, I'd layered a pink top over a blue T-shirt and put on my favourite, frothy orange ballet skirt. Tulip always wears shorts when she's here. The first time she was over I was trying to help her fit in and gave her a pair of my shorts; ones with dinosaur patches on them. She'd loved them so much, now I buy shorts specially for her, customise them and I always sew on dinosaur patches. When we're out explorin', she doesn't wear her own skirts or dresses because people would instantly know she was different so she raids my wardrobe for tops because we're almost the same size.

We still don't look anyway near like other girls our age, she always has twigs and flowers in her hair and when Mum isn't about I take out all the clips and pins from my own hair and let it go wild; which is really wild. We only wear shoes when we're at my house or going somewhere in town, otherwise we go barefoot. Before I met Tulip, I'd never have gone without something on my feet but now I'm used to it, my feet are tough and I prefer it that way.

Mr. Lindsay is used to us so he wasn't fazed by the appearance of two wild girls in his farmyard.

'Are you ready, got everything you need?' he asked.

I nodded.

'The address Becca gave you?'

Mrs. Lindsay has friends who live on our route, they've been really kind and said we could stay overnight and they've offered to let us have some feed for the horses so we didn't need to carry a week's supply with us.

'Thank you, yes, that's brilliant, it'll make it easier not carrying a big load,' I said.

'You really haven't got much, are you sure you'll be okay?' he asked.

We each had a small rucksack to carry the essentials.

'We'll forage for food,' Tulip explained, 'and we'll build shelters when we need them.'

'We've got rain jackets just in case, but hopefully the good weather will last,' I added

'You might need some cash for an emergency,' he held out

a twenty-pound note.

'That's really kind,' I said, 'but mum slipped me some, so we should be okay and we've got a fully charged phone.'

He gave it to us anyway.

'People complain about kids today and their lack of initiative,' he said 'what a nerve!'

Gerry, one of the farm staff was passing and chipped in, 'got me to thank,' he claimed, 'taught them all I know!'

'Gerry, if the chippy was closed for a day you'd starve!' I pointed out.

'Hmmmfph!' he protested.

'Course he wouldn't,' said Mr. Lindsay, 'the curry house does deliveries!'

'We could teach you and then when you're out working in the fields you could find your dinner there too,' offered Tulip. 'It'd be totally healthy and save you lots of money.'

'That would be great … if only I had the time to take you up on your offer …' Gerry sighed.

'Yeah, yeah …' I countered.

Mrs. Lindsay came out to say goodbye.

'Have a great time you two,' she said. 'I'm looking forward to hearing all about it.'

'Lori has found some great places to explore,' said Tulip, 'I'm totally excited about exploring new countryside.'

"Totally" was Tulip's current go-to word, she'd overheard Gus saying it about some TV show and now she was using it all the time.

Finn gave a neigh and nudged me; he was ready to get

going.

'Off you go then,' Mrs. Lindsay said and gave us each a hug.

We mounted and set off.

Day 1
Chapter 2

I had the general direction planned and had picked out some places to explore but otherwise we were going to take things as they came. Our first stop was going to be a shelter we'd built the year before. It was a day's walk but on horseback we'd be there before lunch.

We walked down the road, went through the gate to the water meadow and then had a little canter. Finn and Oliver had been pretty lazy for the last couple of weeks so we'd agreed not to push them until they were a bit fitter. It didn't matter if we took our time, we had plenty to talk about so it was good to have time to chat.

We left our village behind, went through Sovereign Wood and on the other side came across two people out foraging.

I said a cheery, 'hello.'

The man looked up, glared fiercely and turned away. The lady smiled but didn't say anything.

He didn't need to be like that when I was just being friendly so I rode on, Tulip was about to follow but saw he was picking a mushroom and stopped.

'You shouldn't pick that one,' she cautioned.

The man stood up straight and stared at her for a moment. 'Shove off you scaggy traveller, don't you tell ME what to do!'

'I'm not telling you what to do!' Tulip snapped back.

'CLEAR OFF!' he yelled.

'WHAT! I'm just warning you, it looks like Caesars but it's not and it's actually pretty poisonous …'

'I'll not be lectured by some travelling monkey, if you paid your bloody taxes and dressed properly, I might listen to you.'

'I don't need to dress like a boring person to know if something is bad for you,' retorted Tulip.

That made the man even more angry, 'we don't need you poking your nose in when it's not been asked for!'

Tulip was about to give him a piece of her mind and she doesn't hold back, 'you big, fat doddypoll …' she started.

'Hey, look at the time,' I interrupted, 'we'd better get on.'

'But he …' she saw my look and grudgingly nudged Oliver into a trot.

'This is what I think of your damn meddling,' the man shouted after us and to our horror bit into the mushroom he was holding, chewed and swallowed.

'WHAT! How could you be so stupid after she warned you!' I yelled. 'Miss you should phone for an ambulance,' I said to the lady.

'SHOVE OFF!' yelled the man.

'I mean it Miss.'

'JUST GO BACK TO YOUR FLEAPIT!'

'Don't you talk to her like that, you …' Tulip started to turn Oliver round.

I got Finn in her way. 'We're going,' I said firmly and we moved off.

Still even if he was being horrid, I didn't like to think of him getting ill so I called back to the woman, 'Miss, if you keep a hold of the rest of the mushroom then you can show it to the doctor!'

The man swore again and shook his fist.

Just then a small flock of pigeons rose up out of the long grass giving the horses a start and distracting us, by the time we'd settled them we were well away from the shouty man.

As the sun rose, it started to get warmer and the mist began to burn off the fields. It made everything look mystical and a long way from the 21st century. My plan was to stay away from roads and houses as much as we could. It was more fun to stay in the countryside and we didn't want too many people to see Tulip. You can understand, I mean although she looks almost like us, she is an actual goblin. When she came over the second time we discovered this weird thing, which turns out to be really useful. If Tulip meets someone and they don't find out her name they won't remember her, even if they remember me. We still try to keep away from people so we don't have to answer the sort of awkward questions they ask; like where she lives, what school she goes to or what her mum and dad do.

A drovers' road wound up into the hills, we headed for that and as we started to climb, we heard the sound of an ambulance siren.

'They've got to him pretty quickly,' I said. 'How dangerous was that mushroom?'

Tulip shook her head, 'it's bad, it could kill him … if it doesn't, he'll be really sick for a couple of weeks at least.'

'How stupid was he? I mean even if he thought we were

travellers that's no reason not to listen to advice.'

'Why doesn't he like travellers?' Tulip asked.

'God knows. In fact, I bet he's not even met one. He's probably read something on the internet from someone with a grudge and then him and his friends believe it without checking. At school we're always told to do a bit of research because any half-wit can put up stuff online even when it's a load of rubbish.'

'That's why I always check with your mum and dad if you tell me anything,' Tulip claimed.

I didn't take the bait. 'If a traveller told me not to eat a mushroom, I'd believe them, I mean, they're far more likely to know what they're talking about when it comes to foraging than someone like that man.'

After an hour we came to a small stream running across the track so we stopped. There was plenty of lush grass, we let the horses drink and graze and sat dandling our feet in the cool water. Back home Tulip can drink water straight from the streams but over here we have to be more careful so I'd brought a water filter along just to be sure we didn't get any bugs.

'Read to me,' demanded Tulip.

'You can read, shouldn't you be practising and reading to me?'

'But you're so good, you can do all the special voices, like when the animals talk, I don't have a clue what all the different creatures sound like, I mean I've never even seen an elephant or a kangaroo let alone heard them so I can't speak like they do.'

'I don't know either, I make them up,' I pointed out.

'Pleas Lori, pleeease … please read to me,' she wheedled.

'We can't stay too long,' I pointed out.

'I know but just a little bit.'

I'd brought a couple of books so I started the first one.

At the end of the first chapter, I closed the book, 'okay time to go,' I said.

We walked alongside the horses for the first half a mile gathering berries and edible stalks for our lunch. It was getting hot and the white chalk of the path was dazzling and reflected the sun back at us.

When we remounted, Finn showed off and cantered ahead, Oliver wasn't interested and kept ambling along at a trot even though Tulip really wanted to race. We slowed down to let them catch us up and I rubbed it in that we were fastest.

'We took our time … we wanted to enjoy the countryside, 'she claimed. 'We saw loads of interesting things while you were dashing about like a white-toothed shrew and you missed them all.'

'Like what? What did you see?'

'We saw … we saw a mountain hare, a red kite …'

'Yeah?'

' … a totally cool strawman … he asked if your pants were on fire and were you trying to find a cold pond to stick your bum in?'

'Finn and I love going fast, it's the biggest thrill ever,

bigger even than meeting a talking scarecrow,' I retorted.

We jumped a wall and that was us on the moor. In the distance lots of sheep were grazing. We stayed quiet, kept low on the horses and steered them towards the flock.

'Make sure you don't try and count them in case you fall asleep,' I whispered to Tulip and she just said us humans have the maddest ideas.

There were hundreds and they were really beautiful, wild coats, curly horns and big bright eyes. As we got closer, they stopped grazing and looked up.

Finn and Oliver gave them a sniff but they aren't interested in sheep and walked on.

A couple of the ewes stood up and wandered out of our way but the rest stared for half a minute or so and then went back to grazing.

The horses delicately stepped through the middle of the flock, pausing every now and then to take a mouthful of grass.

Tulip and I looked at each other and we almost giggled with pleasure, how good was this, we were close enough to the sheep we could stretch down and stroke them.

'I can't believe we walked right through the middle,' agreed Tulip. 'Oliver and Finn must have magic powers I wonder if we could go through any flock or herd?'

'I've got magic powers too, I walked through a herd of wild cows when I was ten,' I reminded her.

'Yeah, but you were covered in mud and stuff so they probably thought you were a walking swamp ...'

'A SWAMP! I looked adorable, they saw how beautiful I was and were entranced … in fact those sheep probably thought the same, they wanted to stay and admire me and that's why they didn't run away.'

She laughed, 'you mean me!'

'They saw you and thought look at the giant thistle on top of that horse, yummm tasty!'

'Thistles have crowns, so I'm the queen of you!' she retorted.

I sarcastically said, 'of course your majesty!'

'You still have to do what I say, "Swampy girl"!'

We wandered through the familiar countryside exchanging insults until we came to a fork in the road. Down the left path, just visible, was the tower of a castle.

'Can we go and look this time,' asked Tulip.

All the other times we've come here, it's been on foot and we always felt the castle was too far out of our way. Today with the horses we could be there and back really quickly so I said, 'yeah let's'.

It turned out it wasn't a castle but an old church, the pointy steeple part of the tower had fallen down and the stones were lying about the graveyard. The main door was gone, all the glass from the windows was missing, the stone pulpit was in place but the pews and everything else had been taken away.

'Hey, there's a cave underneath,' said Tulip, 'come on!'

'It's not a cave, it's a crypt,' I corrected her, '… it looks scary.'

'It does not Lori,' she was already halfway down and I reluctantly followed, I wanted to be sure she was okay … and I didn't want to be a wuss.

It was pretty fusty and gloomy, a lot colder than outside and it smelt dank. Around the walls were big, stone coffins, skeletons had been carved on some of them and they all had plaques on the top.

'Look at all the skulls and bones, spooky, why are these boxes down here?' Tulip asked.

'This is where they put people's bodies…'

'There are bodies inside?' she went up and put her hands on the top. 'Really?'

Now we were in the crypt, the creepy shadows didn't bother me so much.

'Rich people were buried in big coffins like these, in those days.' I read out some of the names on the tombs; 'Cleophes Reaney; Paston Reaney; Dove Reaney; Bethshien Ardrey. This must be the Reaney family church. I wonder where the village was?'

'We'll look for it when we're done here …'

'Okay,' I agreed.

'Is that funny smell the people?' she asked.

'I don't think so, they were buried here hundreds of years ago.'

She tapped one of the stone coffins, 'perhaps they'll come back to life?'

'That would be impossible …'

'But …'

'Impossible,' I repeated. 'They'll have rotted away to nothing by now!'

'What's that sound?' she cupped her ear. '"CREEEEAKKK" oh my goodness they're WAKING UP!' She clutched my arm and shook it, 'look Lori, the lids are moving, any second now they'll push them off and sit up. When they do they'll be all rotten, their bones will be sticking out and their faces will have been eaten away by worms …'

'Gross!'

'"WE'RE COMING TO GET YOU!"' She turned and walked, stiff-armed and lurching like her legs didn't bend. '"WHO ARE YOU? WHAT ARE YOU DOING HERE?"' she said in a deep, scary voice, '"WHY HAVE YOU DISTURBED US?"'

'What do you want?' I asked, pretending to shudder.

'"WE WANT REVENGE!"' she intoned.

'Revenge?' I said sceptically. 'Hang on a sec, Mr Cleophes died when he was seventy-eight, that's a pretty good age if you lived in those times, what could he possibly want revenge for?'

'I don't know, someone stood on his bad toe, his breakfast toast was burnt to a cinder, his best hat was stolen …' Tulip persisted. '"REVENGE, REVENGE, I will have my RE-VEEEENGE!!!!"' she chanted.

'And why would he be bothered with us? We don't know him, we don't even come from here and we didn't step on his toe!'

'That's what dead people do when they wake up … they're

confused and angry so they lash out at anyone nearby,' she decided.

'But they might have been really nice people and if they did somehow come back to life, they might just want to make us a cup of tea, give us a piece of cake and have a chat about how things have changed,' I suggested.

She lurched about a bit more, grunting loudly. 'No, they'd be ROARING, STORMING ZOMBIES!'

'Yeah?'

'Indeed so!'

'Tulip, they will not.'

She stuck her tongue out, 'they will. Anyway, time to find the village … maybe there'll be pirates there.'

'Pirates, why Tulip?'

She ignored my question and just said 'come on!'

It had been very dry recently so we could see the faint marks of the road curving away from the church. We followed it for half a mile to a stone cross, beyond it was the village. It would have been a pretty sizeable place, there were lots of cottages and quite a few barns; some of the buildings were just walls but a fair few still had roofs.

'How sad,' said Tulip wistfully.

We dismounted and wandered along the abandoned street.

I shaded my eyes and looked around, 'a bit of a lack of pirates, Tulip!' I said pointedly.

She ignored me. 'That's where the big house was,' she crossed the street to an overgrown hedge. 'The garden wall is under this. I wonder what made them leave?'

'I dunno, pirates?'

'It's lovely site, good soil for crops and fresh water nearby.'

'Maybe the rich people got bored living in the country or the workers moved to the city because the wages were better, perhaps the jobs in the town were easier … OR … perhaps they left and signed up to be pirates! Is this a gatepost?' I added.

The ivy leaves moved out of the way for Tulip so we could see it more clearly.

'Reaney Lodge,' she read aloud.

We went into the garden to check if anything was left of the house, the garden was just weeds, some straggly hedges and a lot of old fruit trees. The apples weren't ripe, the plums and cherries had all been eaten by the birds and the pears were tiny and rock hard. The house itself wasn't a house anymore but you could see it must have been amazing. The front was still there up to the top of the ground floor windows, we could see the shape of the rooms and some of the chimneys rose up above the ruined walls. At the back was a solid building that looked like a cold store, it still had a roof but the door was long gone.

We couldn't tell whether the house had been knocked down, burnt down or just fallen down.

'I thought there'd have been more than just bits of wall …' said Tulip.

'You were hoping pirates would be camping out in the grounds, after their ship had been blown here in a huge storm …'

'Lori!' she sighed as if I was an idiot, 'that would be impossible …'

I gave her a look.

'Come on don't dawdle, let's get on,' said Tulip and turned back to the horses.

We remounted and didn't stop until we got to our camp.

'Our den's looking good,' I said as we inspected the shelter.

The last time we'd been here we'd cut turf and laid it on the roof and the sidewalls. The grass had grown well, so from the outside it just looked like a grassy knoll, while the inside was dry and cosy.

'I'll check the hooves for stones,' offered Tulip.

She gave them a once over, I tidied the inside, swept away the cobwebs and collected dry wood.

Once the chores were done, Tulip wanted to race. There was a huge loch nearby so we decided to go there.

We called to Finn and Oliver.

'Come on we're going for a swim …' beckoned Tulip.

'On … your … marks …' I left a long pause to try and catch Tulip off guard, 'getsetGO!' I said in a rush.

We sprinted off and the horses followed, curious to see where we were going. Half way there I pretended I was getting tired, slowed down and dropped back, Tulip relaxed thinking she'd won and I put on a spurt and raced past.

'Hey!' she complained.

She had to work hard and only just caught up as we got to the little beach.

We didn't stop and ran straight into the water. It was deliciously cool after such a hot day.

Finn followed us, prancing around biting the water and generally acting the fool.

'Hey Oliver, come on in,' I called, but he stayed at the side paddling sedately.

'He's like my Aunty Marigold,' Tulip suggested, 'she just sits on the bank looking smug and never gets anything but her feet wet!'

We splashed Oliver and he gave us a long-suffering look.

Tulip and I ducked, dived and splashed each other. We pretended we were mermaids and we had to keep our treasure safe from greedy pirates who were too lazy to go out and plunder properly. The pirates tried to sneak up in their rowing boat and we led them on a wild goose chase until eventually one of the brighter ones said, 'ahoy mateys, we're 'a' going round in circles.'

'AAARH,' roared Tulip, 'rattle my compass so we are.'

'Maybe there ain't no treasure, captain, and I've a fearsome rumble in me belly,' I complained in my best pirate accent.

Now we were the pirates. We gave up hunting for gold, rowed back to our ship and shouted to the cook for beer and "skull and cross-buns".

'Hoist the oven gloves,' called Tulip.

'Splice the main chips,' I added.

The talk of food made us think about dinner too and it was time to head back to camp.

'You go on, I'll catch us a fish,' offered Tulip.

'That'd be great.' I left her to it and took the horses back. I groomed them and checked for cuts or grazes so by the time she was back, the salt lick was set up, Finn and Oliver were contentedly eating the feed we'd brought along and the fire was lit.

We'd brought cotton bags, so we filled them with dry grass to sleep on and then cooked the fish.

It was a perfect evening, we ate our dinner watching the sun set, I read a bit more of our book out loud and when it got too dark, we chatted and watched the fire sparking. Eventually it was bedtime, we dampened down the fire and slipped into the shelter to sleep.

Day 2
Chapter 1

'You asleep Lori,' Tulip asked, giving me a shove to make sure I wasn't.

'Not any more you pest …'

I opened my eyes the first rays of sun were peeking through our little stick door.

'I had a really good sleep, so your snoring didn't keep me awake …' she said.

'I don't snore,' I corrected her.

'I thought Finn had stuck his head in the door it was so loud!'

'Yeah?'

'Yeah!' She stretched and wiggled her fingers. 'I had a dream last night.'

'What about?'

'About those people in the church, the Reaney family,' she said.

'Was it a good dream?'

'Sort of. What you said about how they might have been nice people must have stuck in my head.'

I sat up and wiped the sleep from eyes. 'What happened?'

'Is my hair okay?' she turned so I could check the back.

I fluffed it up.

'Thanks. In my dream I wasn't in the den, I was in one of the cottages but it was like it was when it was new. You were with me, actually you're always with me in dreams, and we were dressed up in big dresses like they are in your picture books of the olden days. Mr. and Mrs. Reaney drove up in a big, fancy carriage with four horses!'

'Four horses, that's pretty grand,' I suggested.

'They invited us round for tea, their footman helped us up and then drove us to their house. It was huge, almost a castle, all white, dazzling in the sun and around it was the loveliest garden. The trees were young, they looked perfect and their branches were laden with fruit. Mrs. Reaney took us to the most beautiful room of them all, laid out on the table were big jugs of lemonade, tons of sandwiches, loads of cakes and even a plate of Freddoes!'

'Freddoes?'

'It was a dream,' she pointed out. 'We were chatting away quite the thing, like we were best mates, when suddenly Mr. Cleophes looked sad. I asked him what was wrong.'

'Did he say?'

She gave a wistful look, 'Yes, he said soon he'd be dead and his house would gone and no one would ever remember him or his family. I said I would and then I asked what would happen to the house. He said he didn't know. Then we were standing outside the gate, like we were yesterday, and the house was gone.'

'Oh.'

'So I never found out. It happens a lot on this side, doesn't it?' she said sadly.

'You mean buildings disappearing ...'

'Yes, people leave, their houses fall down and then just disappear.'

'Like I said, for anyone living somewhere remote it must have been difficult, no doctors if you were ill, no shops if you wanted new pots and pans and you had to travel for hours to get anywhere. I mean it took us a whole day to get here, imagine what it would have been like for your gran if she'd lived in that village and she needed something she couldn't make for herself, like she broke her teapot or her best pan, how would she get a new one?'

'S'pose …'

'Hey cheer up, Tulip. If we worry about all the things that have gone, we're never going to enjoy ourselves.'

'I know it was a dream but it made me sad.'

I gave her a hug. 'They might have come into a fortune, bought themselves a house next to a fun park, then all their friends moved in next door and they had loads of horses and went riding every day. You know maybe they're only buried here because they asked to be buried where they were born, people do that you know.'

We crawled out of our bivvy and Oliver and Finn whinnied to say good morning … actually I'm making that up, they did whinny but they might have been telling us off for getting up late and complaining how they'd been ready for hours!

It hardly took any time to pack and we were soon on our way.

Day 2
Chapter 2

We were going to camp again tonight and the next night we'd be staying with Mrs. Lindsay's friends.

We wanted to find a place to camp nice and early to give us time to build a shelter so we didn't bother with breakfast and foraged on the way.

'Here you go, this is yummy,' Tulip handed me a stalk I never seen before. She was right, it had a lovely sweet flavour.

We reached the "Crow Post", we call it that because the first time we saw it a rowdy murder of crows were squabbling over who got to sit on the top. We'd not been any further than here, so from now on it would be all new countryside.

Tulip pointed to the hills in the distance, 'I bet there are wild things in those mountains!'

'You reckon?'

'Out in the backwoods you have to watch out for all sorts fierce creatures.'

'Wolves?'

'Uh-huh.'

'Big, hairy, scary bears …'

'Yes …'

'Giant eagles with beaks like knives, stinky, bug-ridden hedgehogs, sharp-toothed wildcats?' I suggested.

'YES!' she agreed and then told me off because hedgehogs are her particular favourites. 'You shouldn't be horrid about hedgehogs, they're lovely, friendly, hard-working, no-nonsense sorts of fellows.'

'They're just buses for fleas,' I teased.

She just raised her eyes to the sky and tutted at my disparaging remark. 'We'll need to be armed and ready ...' she decided.

We each found a long straight branch that would do as a spear and marched beside the horses, eyes peeled and on high alert.

Something rustled in the hedgerow.

'A hungry wolf!' whispered Tulip.

We thrust our spears out in front, ready in case of trouble.

A red squirrel scurried out of the bushes, stopped in the middle of the path and started gnawing at a nut he'd found.

'Watch out for those teeth, the fiercest creature in the forest,' I murmured.

Oliver snorted, the squirrel did a funny double take and then scampered away as if its tail was on fire.

'We're lucky he didn't attack, he could have nibbled our ankles,' I said, pretending to wipe my brow.

'A lucky escape,' Tulip agreed. 'Did you know boys are scared of squirrels?' she asked.

'I didn't, why?'

'Because squirrels are always on the lookout for nuts to chew!'

'TULIP! You are so rude!' I pretended to tell her off, but I couldn't keep a straight face and started laughing.

She laughed too then she was serious, 'what's that?'

'What?'

'Over there, it's a rotten, princess-eating, house-tromping, chocolate-hoarding dragon. YOU'LL NEVER GET AWAY WITH STEALING OUR CHOCOLATE, YOU MAY RUN BUT YOU CAN'T ESCAPE!' yelled Tulip and shook her spear. She leapt on Oliver and urged him into a canter, 'THE CHASE IS ON!' she called to me and Finn.

I sprang on Finn, he didn't need any encouragement and raced after Oliver and Tulip. We didn't want the horses to overdo it so we reined them in after a bit, let them cool down and eventually stopped at a stream.

'I think we've frightened Mr Dragon off,' I said, 'I shall have to have a word with his mum about his poor, antisocial behaviour. I mean he ate a whole village with his mouth open, yuck!'

'You don't chat with their mums,' she declared, 'you have to teach them a lesson in one-to-one combat. HA! HA! HAAA!' she bellowed and waved her spear about in what she thought looked like cool spear-handling moves.

'I can't tell if you're fighting a dragon or a frog has jumped down your front,' I said.

'I'm a warrior princess,' she retorted, 'these are the super-special skills I learnt in warrior princess school.'

While the horses grazed, we paddled across to a little rock in the middle of the stream and sat in the sun lunching on the berries we'd collected.

Finn and Oliver must have felt safe because they took it in turn to snooze. We stayed a couple of hours to give them a chance to properly relax.

'You know, if we were really hunting something … say a lion or a tiger, I'd only want to say hello,' said Tulip.

'Maybe from a distance, they're fierce you know.'

'Yes … and because I wouldn't want to eat a tiger …'

'I can't think they'd taste nice anyway,' I suggested. 'Things that don't taste nice often have black and yellow stripes don't they, like wasps and bees?'

'Have you tasted a wasp?'

'Yuck no, I wonder how people ever found out they don't taste nice. I mean I've just been told; I don't know for sure.'

'I bet they had to draw lots,' suggested Tulip. 'If you picked number one you had to taste an apple, pick number two and you tasted an anemone, number three it was an ant and so on until they'd gone through everything in the world and tasted everything.'

'There'd have been some revolting things and a lot of stuff is poisonous, imagine if you were the one who had to try Belladonna! "Yum very nice, sweet but it's got a bit of a kick …" you'd say before keeling over dead …'

'I suppose at least the rest of them knew it was bad. The man doing the experiment would make a note in his little book. "Don't eat Belladonna berries, now what have we here", he'd have said, "Monkshood that's a pretty flower I'm sure this will be fine, here you go Phinchas, a nice little salad for you …'

'I don't think they'd have got a lot of volunteers once word got out,' I pointed out.

'Obviously they wouldn't tell people what they were doing, they'd have asked for people to come and taste chocolate and nice stuff like cakes and buns, there'd be a queue out the door and then they'd say "while you're here have a nibble of this".'

Finn and Oliver both started to amble about, they'd had enough of a rest and we remounted and headed off.

We had a long discussion about food tasting because it must have been tricky before they knew for sure what was good and what would make you ill or even kill you. I mean, take that man picking the mushrooms, he obviously thought he knew his stuff; and some mushrooms are fine but there are others that if the tiniest bit touches your lips, you're dead as a doornail.

We were so occupied coming up with brilliant ideas for how they tested what you could eat, before we knew it, we were on a tarmac road and ahead was a row of houses.

Day 2
Chapter 3

'What's the smell?' Tulip asked as we went down the hill.

I stopped Finn and took a big sniff.

'It's an awful stink,' said Tulip.

'You know I think it's a gas leak,' I decided.

'It's almost as bad as Buckweed's dog and he's the worst smelling thing ever. What's gas?'

'It's a fuel; people heat their houses and cook with it.'

The horses started to get jittery so they didn't like the smell much either.

'When I was in Primary Seven, we had a day out with the police and the fire people,' I remembered. 'The firemen told us you have to be specially careful if there's a gas leak, in case it explodes …'

'EXPLODES!' Tulip said, 'we'd better warn the people who live here then.'

The smell was strongest at the big house in the middle of the row, I slipped off Finn and opened the gate. The man from the fire brigade had explained any sort of spark could set the gas alight …you know even from a light switch or a doorbell so I carefully knocked on the front door.

There was no answer.

'No one at home,' I called to Tulip.

'I'll check the two houses back up the way,' she offered.

I warned her how the tiniest spark can make the gas

explode so to be extra, extra careful and then I went down to the next cottage.

A lady came to the door, she had two children with her. She looked suspicious when she saw me – I suppose my full wild child look can be a bit unexpected.

'Er hi … er we thought we'd better warn you …'

'Warn us?' she asked sharply.

'Yes, there's a real strong smell of gas coming from the house next door.'

One of the kids wandered into the garden, 'Mummy look at the lovely horse …' then she got a whiff of the gas, 'what's that stinky stink …'

The lady sniffed. 'You're right that's really bad. Come back Emily,' she called to the girl. 'Thank you,' she said to me in a softer tone.

'It's a whole lot worse up the road maybe we should phone the gas people,' I suggested.

'Yes, we'd better but I think we should go further away,' she decided. 'Don't touch any of the switches,' she warned the girl.

I explained we'd knocked on the door of the next-door house but there was no one in.

'Mrs. Grier lives in the big house; she'll be at work.'

'Will your other neighbours be in?' I asked.

'The couple next door are on holiday, but Sarah Grant is at home with her baby, she's in the last house in the row.'

'He's a ginormous horse,' the girl said, 'is he friendly?'

'He's very friendly, you can stroke him if you like. Hey

Finn,' I said. He bent his head down so the girl could stroke his nose.

'His fur is very soft,' she said.

'It's lovely, isn't it? I'll go and say to Mrs. Grant, my friend has gone up the hill to say to the people there.'

'We'll come with you,' the lady decided, 'just let me grab my phone and bag.'

By the time she was ready, Tulip was walking back down and talking to a man.

'Can you smell it Mary?' the man asked. 'I think we'd best get down the hill pronto and phone from there.'

'Come on you two,' she said and hustled the children along.

I knocked on Mrs. Grant's door.

'Who are you?' she asked, I think she was about to tell me to push off, then she saw the man and Mary.

'Mrs. Lamont, Lorne, what's going on?'

'There's a gas leak Sarah, we going down to the village to phone from there,' said the man. 'Don't switch on any lights, probably best not to touch anything.'

'Is it poisonous … the baby?'

'I don't think it's poisonous,' I said.

'Not outside anyway,' added the man.

'The baby will be fine Sarah,' added Mrs. Lamont, 'but I think we should go.'

Tulip was saying hello to Emily and asking her where she got her doll.

'Granny gave it to me,' the little girl said.

'It's lovely,' said Tulip and asked its name.

'She's called Bonbon, Granny says she's a sweetie … like me.'

Mrs. Grant grabbed a bag of baby things, locked the front door and followed us.

'Is gas bad Mummy?' Emily asked.

'NO … no it's fine, we're just being careful,' her mother replied.

'Do you like horses,' I asked to distract her.

'Yeah, I rode a little one when we were on holiday …'

'You could ride Finn with me,' I suggested, 'if your mum doesn't mind.'

The lady nodded so I mounted.

'How did you get up there?' the girl asked, eyes as big as saucers.

'Practice,' I said and reached down.

Tulip gave her boost and we sat her in front of me.

'We're so high! Hey her horse is even bigger,' she announced when Tulip brought Oliver up. 'Does she have the bigger horse because she's better than you?'

'No … she's useless, I'm the best' I said.

Tulip laughed.

'HOUSEY!' her brother stuck his pudgy little finger out and pointed at Finn.

'Horsey,' his mum corrected.

'You're very wild children,' the man commented, 'where are you from …'

'LORNE DUNCAN!' the lady admonished him.

'That's okay Mrs. Lamont. We do look wild,' I admitted, 'but only when we're out adventuring.' I showed them my school picture; I always carry it so I can show people we're actually quite respectable.

'Is this really you?' the lady asked, when she saw me neat as a new pin in my school uniform.

I nodded. 'In the holidays we're allowed to run free. We usually stay closer to home but a friend lent us her horses so we've come a bit further. It's a brilliant opportunity to practice our Duke of Edinburgh skills, you know live off the land and stuff.'

'That's very brave,' Mr. Duncan said warmly, I think seeing the picture had reassured him we weren't tearaways or thieves.

'It's great getting to see new places,' added Tulip.

They asked about our exploring and we explained how we liked being as far away from people, from the cities and the traffic as we could go. 'When we're out, we stay ever so still and the birds and animals don't notice you're there.'

'What sort of animals? Mrs. Grant asked.

'All sorts,' explained Tulip, 'weasels, stoats, rabbits, hares, dragonflies, grass snakes, otters and plenty of deer. We were in a spinney once, a couple of grouse walked past, they came so close we could have touched them.'

I agreed, 'there's an amazing number of wild creatures and actually they live much closer to people than you'd imagine. It's just they stay out of sight, or only come out at night.'

We were halfway down the hill when Mr. Duncan spotted

a van. 'That's a bit of luck there's a gas van at the Dollman's. I wonder if they've already had a phone call?'

We hurried to where it was parked and Mr. Duncan knocked on the window. When the man wound it down, he explained about the gas leak.

'Gas leak? We're just installing a boiler. Was it a strong smell?'

'Yes, really strong,' Mrs Grant said.

'Pooh! Horrid,' confirmed Emily holding her nose.

The man and his mate got out of their van.

'Horrid eh?' said the mate. 'That's sounds bad miss.'

Emily nodded, 'very bad.'

'Whereabouts then?' asked the one in charge.

His mate obviously knew his way around horses because he came over, greeted Oliver and patted his flank. 'You're a fine looking fellow,' he said and Oliver gave a little whinny of agreement.

Mr. Duncan pointed up the hill, 'there's just the one road up to our houses,' he said.

'We don't have the tools, we'll have to phone the office,' the senior workman explained. 'Any one still up there?'

'We're all out, the neighbours are either on holiday or at work,' Mr Duncan confirmed

'Good, we'll seal off the road. No one is to go up there because even turning on a light can be enough of a spark and then BOOM!'

He moved his van, parked it across the road and went to phone. His mate fetched a roll of tape that said "Danger. Do

Not Cross" and stretched it from one lamppost to another.

The first workman came back. 'They'll be here as soon as they can. They'll have to turn the mains gas off down here before they can do anything, so when you go back you won't have any heating or hot water.'

'Oh … oh dear, do you think it'll take long,' the lady with the baby asked.

'They'll get it sorted as soon as possible but they won't know until they find where the leak is.'

Mr. Duncan asked how the emergency team would find the leak, the man was explaining when a big Mercedes pulled up and the driver beeped her horn.

'Oh … Mrs. Grier … she's back early …' Mrs. Lamont said and I could tell from her expression she didn't much like the new lady. In fact I don't think Mr. Duncan or Mrs. Grant liked her either.

The horn beeped again and Finn got fidgety at the noise. We explained to Mrs. Lamont how the horses didn't like loud noises and anyway we should get on.

As the horn hadn't made anyone move, the lady got out of her car. 'Let me through, I'm in hurry …' she demanded.

She was pretty enough, smartly dressed and her hair was very shiny but I wouldn't want to be friends with her.

'We'd better go,' I said and together Tulip and I helped Emily down. 'It was lovely to meet you all, I hope it gets sorted quickly.'

'Thank you for stopping and warning us,' said Mr. Duncan and Mrs. Grant and Mrs. Lamont said thank you too.

'Bye Emily,' said Tulip and we waved as we trotted off.

When we were out of hearing Tulip said she didn't like the new lady. 'I bet she always wants to get her own way, like she's the only one who matters, she looks like a big bully to me!'

I agreed. 'Anyway, we've done our good deed for today, everyone is safe, nothing blew up and the gas people will sort it out for them.'

'Where now?' Tulip asked.

'We've got maybe a couple of hours riding before we start looking for a good camping spot but there's plenty of time so we can still stop and explore places if we want.

About half a mile out of the village we passed a house. It was like the builders had got halfway through and then stopped. The roof was on, but there was glass in the windows and no doors. Weeds were growing everywhere, on the roof, in the rooms and the garden was overgrown. On the pathway to the front door were bunches of dead flowers, a wreath and some bedraggled teddy bears and dolls.

We dismounted to have a look. There were message tags on the flowers but they must have been there for ages because the writing was mostly washed away and we couldn't read anything.

'The people must have died,' suggested Tulip. She pointed to the toys, 'the children too?'

'I suppose ...'

It wasn't dark and spooky like the crypt, it was just a half-finished house. We're always exploring ruins, we've been in plenty of mysterious places but this time neither of us wanted to even look in, it felt a really, really sad place.

We mounted the horses, wheeled them round and trotted away without looking back.

Day 2
Chapter 4

As we made our way across the moors to the next camp there were plenty of interesting things to see; a big stone sheepfold with a shepherds' hut at one end, the walls were in perfect condition but the inside of the fold was completely overgrown with brambles so it can't have been used for years; two wooden railway carriages were sitting next to a small loch, they were a bit bashed about as cows had been using them for shelter; we rode over an ancient, hump-backed footbridge, on one of the parapets was a carving of a hare, there was writing underneath but we couldn't tell what it said as it was so weatherworn and then in the middle of a field was an old wooden rowboat even though we were miles from a lake or river. Finn wanted to examine the boat so we stopped and tried to work out why it was there. It was full of water it wasn't leaking so it was still actually a useable boat. When Finn was ready, we set off again and didn't stop until we reached a wooded valley; I'd found it on the internet, it was a long way from any houses or roads so I thought it would be a good place to spend the night.

'Well done, this is lovely,' said Tulip. 'Look there's a stream too.'

We split up to look for potential sites for a den.

'Lorelei …' she was coming out from under the trees.

'Uh-huh?' I went back.

'I think we'd be better to make a sort of house up above … in the branches …'

'Why?'

'Brocks.'

I went across and as I got closer I could see the entrances to badger setts.

'Will the horses be okay? I hadn't planned on hoisting Finn ten feet off the ground.'

'The brocks will ignore them and just get on with their own business but we want to be off the ground, because we don't want them coming into our shelter. They might get a start if we move and if they think we're a threat they might start biting or clawing.'

'I don't like the sound of biting and clawing …'

'Me neither,' she agreed.

We had a second scout around; looking upwards this time.

I spotted a big oak with a wide crown and called Tulip over. 'What about this?'

She shinned up to take a look, 'perfect,' she decided.

Before we built our shelter, we made sure Oliver and Finn were fine, checked hooves, groomed them, sorted the salt lick and the feed. There was plenty of grass around but they were doing a lot more exercise than normal so it was best they had some of their usual food. You could tell they were enjoying themselves, Mrs. Lindsay was right, they'd been getting bored in their field but now their eyes were sparkling, their nostrils were open wide and they were more vocal, snorting when we were riding. Once they were settled, we set to work building a shelter in the tree. We made string from dry stalks, gathered sticks for the roof and cut some flexible branches to help weave things together. Tulip climbed back up the tree, I tied parcels of twigs together and she hauled them up. Once we had enough, I scrambled up after her. The crown was plenty big enough to sleep on and we just needed to make enough of a roof in case it rained. Soon we were done and all we needed was dry grass for our cotton bags.

We had a wash in the stream, sat in the sun to dry off and then foraged for our dinner. There were plenty of berries and shoots and Tulip found some edible mushrooms. I always let her collect the mushrooms because she really knows which are safe.

On our way back to the den we came across a huge tree lying on the ground. There must have been a tremendous storm to rip something so huge right out of the earth. The roots were twice as tall as us and it looked like a giant, gnarly, woody octopus, snaky, twisty arms sticking out in every direction, there were holes in the middle that looked like eyes and below them you could imagine a big wide, mouth full of fangs.

'OH NO! It's the fearsome MONSTER OF THE WOOD!' I said, 'she's protecting the forest from strangers and stops anyone who comes through …'

'What does she want?' Tulip asked.

'You have to solve a riddle before you can go through!' I said and then I roared in my bestest, deepest, most menacing, monster voice, 'ANSWER ME THIS AND I'LL LET

YOU PASS … the more you take, the more you leave behind. What am I?'

The moment I said it I realised Tulip knew the answer, but she pretended to think about it before she answered.

'Footsteps?'

'Yes … well done,' I grudgingly admitted.

It was Tulip's turn, she went behind the tree and thundered, 'I AM THE GREAT GUARDIAN OF THE WOODS, TELL ME… what runs but has no legs?'

'Eeek …' I was about to say "an engine" but of course that couldn't be the answer because it had to be a riddle her friends from home would know and they didn't have a clue about cars or vans or any of those sorts of thing. It wasn't an animal because they have legs and things like snakes and worms don't run.'

'HA-HA-HA, I'LL BE TAKING YOU BACK TO MY UNDERGROUND LAIR AND YOU'LL BE MY SLAVE FOREVER,' she boomed. She pretended to consider things, 'I think I'll have you washing plates and scrubbing pots!' she added.

'Wait, wait …' I looked around for inspiration, I heard the stream splashing away in the distance and the answer came in a flash, 'a stream, no … NO water!'

'Bah …' then she grinned and agreed I was right.

We strolled back to our camp, the forest monster chummed us and asked more riddles. It was okay if we got any wrong now because we'd passed the most important test. There were some good brainteasers but by the time we got back the monster was sharing her favourite jokes.

When it started to get dark, we climbed the tree to our den and watched the sun set.

In the middle of the night Tulip nudged me awake, she had one finger over her mouth and was pointing down with the other hand. The moon was up, the sky was clear and at the foot of the tree a family of badgers were shuffling about, sniffing and checking things. They weren't going near the horses but didn't seem bothered they were there. The boars were larger than I'd expected, I'd never seen one in real life before, just in photos. They looked pretty tough, one of them was making short work of digging a hole looking for worms and bugs. Some of the older ones were dragging bundles of leaves and grass into the undergrowth, the cubs played with each other but were careful not to stray too far from the adults. We stayed as quiet as we could because they'd probably never seen people and we didn't want to spook them.

I looked across to Tulip, she looked so happy and was gazing down fascinated. We watched the badgers for ages before we drifted back to sleep.

Day 3
Chapter 1

The first rays of sun appeared over the horizon, I was the first awake so I poked Tulip. She yawned, stretched and opened her eyes.

'Come on lazy-tot, I've been awake for ages,' I fibbed. 'Where's my breakfast? I'm starving, bacon, eggs and fried mushrooms would be dandy.'

She rooted about in her rucksack.

'You can have my last carrot Lori; I was going to give it to Oliver but my heart would be broken if you starved away to nothingness …'

'Just one left, we need to stock up on carrots then you can have one too.'

'And chocolate, in fact chocolate coated carrots!!' she suggested hopefully. Tulip has had a thing about chocolate from the first day we met so I'd brought a secret stash of Chocolate Freddoes with me.

'No bacon for me, so no chocolate for you! But I do have a bag of mouldy, old Brussels Sprouts … you can have one of them instead.' I dug around in my bag and then gave her one of the Freddoes.

Her eyes lit up and she held it in her hands gazing as if it was a diamond necklace.

'You eat that up,' I said, 'I'll check on the horses. I climbed down and when Finn saw me coming, he gave a whinny of pleasure.

'Morning Finn,' I rubbed his nose and patted his flanks. 'Did you and Oliver sleep well?' I checked round them both to make sure we hadn't missed any cuts or grazes.

'Looks like it going to be a great day,' Tulip came up behind me and gave me a hug.

I brushed a fleck of chocolate from her cheek. 'Didn't take you long to finish that,' I pointed out.

'It's the best,' she sighed with satisfaction. 'Where to today?'

'We're going to stop and say hello to Mrs. Lindsay's friend, Esme, and she said we can sleep there tonight. They've got horses so Finn and Oliver can stay in their stables. Mrs. Lindsay said they've plenty of feed so we can top up and that'll keep us going to the end of the week.'

'Will they be … er … "cool" with us – I mean how we look …'

'I look fine, so they'll be cool with me, you have pictures of dinosaurs on your shorts so they might think you're a bit of a Loopy-Lou.'

'I am not!' Tulip countered in mock outrage. 'I mean look at you, why are you wearing a ballet skirt, even the horses are better at dancing than you?'

'When you dance, people think a bug has crawled down your dress and you're trying to catch it!' I retorted.

'That's so not true, I'm the best dancer in the village, unlike you, when you're dancing you look like a frisky puppy jumping up and down begging for treats!'

Finn gave me a nudge to say "come on"

We collected our rucksacks, mounted and continued our pretend argument as the horses carefully picked their way across the stream.

52

Day 3
Chapter 2

'Becca's friends will be here this afternoon, Keir … you remember?'

'I'm looking forward to meeting them, Esme …'

'Looking forward to checking out the horses, I think!'

'Oh … are they coming on horses?' he asked innocently.

'You know they are. Now Becca warned me the girls are pretty wild so you're not to make any remarks about how they look, no jokes and no critical comments and Becca asked us to try not to ask any personal questions …'

'All teenagers look a shower, I can deal with that.'

'I hope so.'

Her husband went back to his laptop. 'Rona Grier? Name rings a bell …'

'She's that biggity woman, always in the papers boasting how well she's doing. She was in the same year at school as Kenneth; he doesn't have a good thing to say about her.'

'She's back in the news, but I don't think she'll be boasting about it this time …'

Esme glanced over. 'Yes, that's her, what's she done?'

'Blown up her house!'

'No way!'

'Not deliberately,' Keir clarified.

'How?'

'Sounds like she's as stupid as she is biggity. There was a

gas leak on her lane, everyone evacuated and the engineers sealed off the road. Rona Grier turns up and demands to be let through. They don't let her. She insists. They tell her she can't go through yet. An eyewitness told the reporter, "she said … I've got a most important event to attend and I want to shower before I go."'

'She's always got important things to go to and they're always more important than what the rest of us have,' decided Esme.

'Well, they weren't any more impressed with that and told her to move further away. She apparently started muttering to herself, a man from the same row of houses overheard her saying she could at least get the hot water ready for when "the little Hitlers get their act together" and pulled out her phone. As she started fiddling with it, the neighbour realised what she was doing but a moment too late. The daft woman was using an app on the phone to turn her gas boiler on!'

'NO!'

He read out a section from the article. "Seconds later a huge, earth-shattering explosion broke the peace; witnesses looked on in shock as the roof of the house erupted and a massive, acrid, black plume of smoke rose into the sky!"'

'OHMYGOD! Oh … my …god!' Esme gasped.

'Indeed.'

'That's dreadful, I hope no one was hurt.'

'Fortunately they were all far enough away. According to this she's been arrested for causing criminal damage. The gas board managed to turn off the supply and the fire-brigade are now assessing the impact on the other buildings.'

'The poor people who lived next door …'

'Sounds like her neighbours houses were untouched, although the authorities will be checking the structural integrity of each building.'

'Where will they stay?'

'They're being put up in hotels until it's judged safe to go back. Look at the picture!' He enlarged the photo over the whole of the screen to show the smouldering wreck.

'It's completely ruined! How could she be so stupid? I thought everyone knew how dangerous a gas leak is.'

'Probably thought it didn't apply to her, that somehow she was immune to the consequences of her actions.'

Day 3
Chapter 3

My plan was to stay away from towns and villages but we decided to make a detour to the next town to pick up carrots for the horses and we thought we should take a gift for Becca and her husband. I suggested shortbread biscuits but Tulip said that wasn't a treat and insisted we took them chocolates.

The trees started to thin and soon we saw a small town spread out below us.

When we reached the outskirts, Tulip suggested I go down, 'I'll stay and look after the horses,' she said, which was quite sensible of her ... for once.

I tied my hair back, brushed down my t-shirts and skirt so I looked a bit more respectable and made my way into the town. I'm sure I still looked like a new age traveller or something, what with my bare feet and all but I guess so long as I paid my money the shopkeep wouldn't be too fussed.

I stopped at the first store, had a quick scout round and collected what we wanted. The girl on the counter hardly looked at me, asked if I wanted a bag and without waiting for a reply gave me my change.

As I was leaving three boys slouched round the corner; they were a lot older than me, they looked at least eighteen, maybe more.

When they saw me, they started to follow me as I walked

down the road.

'OI!' one of them yelled. 'Wait for us, love …'

'No, leave me alone,' I replied, I kept my head down and walked faster.

The others shouted at me too. They were rude and made horrible suggestions. I walked even quicker and tried to ignore them.

'You a lezzo, then?' said one.

'Look at that hair, not got a brush, eh?' a boy with a weak moustache demanded.

'Smile love, you'd look a lot better!'

'You're a cracker but proper poor if you can't afford shoes!'

'I'll make you straight darling and you can earn some cash too!' the oldest boy said and made a gesture with his hand which I know is very rude.

The others egged him on.

I felt really scared and started running, I just wanted to get back to Tulip, I'd be safe then, no one messes with someone on a horse, specially not a horse as big as Oliver.

They didn't chase after me, just stopped where they were, making horrible suggestions and shouting swears.

I was very glad when I got back to Tulip and the horses.

'Are you okay Lori, you're upset,' she jumped down and gave me a hug.

I was still shivering and explained what had just happened.

'How dare they! What big scaredy chickens, picking on a girl.'

I nodded.

Finn must have sensed I was sad because he came up and rubbed my back with his head.

'What did they say?' she asked.

When I told her, she marched up and down, stomping her feet and growling to herself. 'That's disgusting, skanky tom cats,' she muttered. 'Right, me and Oliver are going to teach them a proper lesson …'

'No … NO we should just leave them,' I said. 'We don't want to risk getting into trouble and having to explain to people.'

She paced up and down a bit more thinking, eventually she stopped being angry and came back to me.

'Okay,' she said. 'I'll let them off this time. They're just stupid boys with big butts. This is them,' she said and paraded up and down, sticking her bum out and doing a funny walk.'

I cheered up watching her.

'And big empty heads,' I said.

'That's because their brains are in their bums.'

'Big floppy bums like puffball mushrooms,' I added.

'Wobble, wobble I'm a fungus,' laughed Tulip and I joined in.

'Feeling better now Lori?'

I nodded.

'Well, if I'm not allowed to let Oliver tromp on them, we should get going,' she said.

Once we were on the outskirts, we gave Finn and Oliver a carrot each and then made our way round the town. We were almost in the country when we heard people shouting.

It was the boys again.

'That's them!' I groaned.

They were in a small paddock at the back of some houses.

We couldn't hear what they were saying but Tulip had had enough.

'Right, you snotty wood lice ...'

I managed to catch her arm before she could nudge Oliver into a trot.

'No, we can't get involved.'

Tulip still had that face ... she was completely fired up, I had to remind her that if we went over and shouted at them, maybe people would hear ...'

'SO ...'

'They might come over to see what's going on ...'

'We'll tell them,' she said, 'we'll tell them about how awful those boys are and what they said to you ...'

'They might want to know your name ...'

'My name? But ...

'Yes.'

'They can't know my name,' she fretted.

'That's why we can't risk it ...' I was interrupted by more shouting, two of the boys started running round the field like they were mad, yelling and acting stupid, the other one wobbled and leant against a tree waving his hand about.

'What are they doing now?' asked Tulip.

'They've probably been drinking, or taking drugs or sniffing glue,' I said.

She asked what that was.

I told her how we'd been to a conference with some girls from other schools, who were all in the same year as us, and the speaker had explained about illegal drugs and that sort of stuff. 'They said people take these drugs because it makes them feel great, like they're flying or having the best time or it makes them think everything looks wonderful and amazing ...'

'Drugs do that?' Tulip asked.

'That's what they said, the lady told us that while sometimes you have a wonderful time, sometimes it's just awful and she said you can't trust the people making the drugs so you don't know which are the ones that are going to make you feel good and ... and well which ones might actually kill you.'

'That's not good, not good at all. There are people at home who drink a lot of cider or Blackthorn wine, they say it makes them happy but I don't know if always does. I've seen grown-ups go totally crazy, they can't stand up or speak properly and they do stupid stuff and look like idiots and those boys look like idiots too.'

The boy leaning against the tree fell over.

'Oh ...' I said.

'He looks poorly,' said Tulip. 'Da's friend got poorly because he drank too much ...'

'Oh poor man ...'

'Uh-huh, Da said he was bouncing about, shouting daft things and laughing a lot then he went quiet and they shouted and called but they couldn't wake him up.'

'And,' I asked.

'Well … well they never did wake him.'

'That's awful,' I said.

'We need to say to someone, those boys could be in trouble like Da's friend,' Tulip said.

I agreed. 'Maybe they are horrid and maybe they are on drugs but that doesn't mean we shouldn't help.' I got my phone out, 'I'll call the police, they'll be able to do something and they'll take them to hospital if they need a doctor.'

I dialled the emergency number, when I got through, they asked where I was and then put me through to the local policeman. I told him about the boys and how they looked ill and how one of them looked the worst.

'Boys?' the man asked.'

I said there were three of them and they'd been horrid to me, I said how I was really frightened, 'I'm only fourteen and the boys are at least eighteen.'

'Tell them to hurry,' interrupted Tulip, 'the boy by the tree has stopped moving.'

I repeated what she'd said and added that the boys really looked like something was wrong with them. 'Maybe they've drunk too much or maybe they've got hold of a bad drug,' I suggested.

The man on the other end of the line listened very carefully. I described where they were and he said there was a police car close by so he was sending them round to check. He said he'd had another report of three young men causing trouble and he was sorry they'd harassed me too. He asked my name, where I lived and my phone number as I might have to give a statement. I said I only had an emergency phone so I wasn't keeping it switched on as I didn't want to use up the battery but I'd be home at the end of the week and gave him our house phone number. He said it was no problem and he would contact me there when I was back.

I'd only just turned the phone off when a police car drove down the road and stopped. The boys didn't notice and kept acting stupid.

The policemen got out their car and went into the field. We didn't wait to see any more. The police would help the boys if they were ill and hopefully tell them off for saying nasty things to me. If they wanted to know what the boys said, I could say "exactly", as I remembered every word.

We headed into the countryside and now we were even more keen to keep away from roads, cars and most especially people. The path looked well-used, the grass was worn down but we didn't meet anyone and then it just sort of ran out and we were in the wilderness again.

Oliver was ready for a gallop and didn't need any encouragement from Tulip, Finn and I followed and we left the town far behind. We passed a few sheep but there weren't any fences or walls.

'It's cool the sheep can wander where ever they want,' decided Tulip when we slowed down.

'Yeah, I bet it's a lot nicer than being stuck in the same field all day.'

'Is it like that when you're at school? Do you feel like

you're a sheep there?' she asked.

'Yes, what a life!' I said. 'We're herded into class by dogs, we have to eat grass for lunch and then they shove us out into the cold at the end of the day!'

'Be serious …'

'And once every six months they put us through the dip.'

'That's just not true!' she contended.

'I suppose it's not like being stuck in a field because you're not doing the same thing all the time, it changes every lesson and in between times we play sports, or make music or do plays or get involved with interesting things like debates or quizzes or clubs.'

'Some of it I'd like,' she decided. 'You know the learning and the games, but I'd hate spending all those hours indoors. I mean even in winter we're outside if it's light because there are always things that need to be done.'

'It's a bummer not being in the fresh air all the time,' I admitted, 'but the learning makes up for it and it's not like it's all day. We don't start 'til nine and even if I've got a club, I'm still away by five o'clock in the afternoon so most of the day is my own anyway.'

The ground started to get boggy on both sides of the trail, Oliver picked his way towards a small coppice and Finn carefully followed in his hoofprints. We were almost at the tree line when Finn stopped and started looking around.

'What's wrong Finn?' I asked.

He moved his head to the left. I couldn't see anything. Tulip pulled Oliver up and looked back to see why we weren't following.

'Finn's worried about something,' I explained.

She listened for a moment, 'it's a sheep bleating,' she said.

I listened too, she was right it didn't sound normal, more like it was upset.

At first, we thought it might have been warning the rest of the flock that we were coming but as we got closer it didn't move. It looked anxious and was shifting nervously as if it wanted to go forward but the ground was too wet and boggy so its feet kept sinking in.

'There's a lamb in there,' Tulip jumped off Oliver and pointed to a little white shape moving weakly.

I got down too.

'We can't just go across,' she decided.

I stepped forward and my foot sank a bit, it was soft and squelchy. 'We'll have to be careful it could be like quicksand and we might get sucked under.'

'We need a bridge then,' she suggested.

'Yeah,' I agreed.

She checked around, 'there's plenty of dead wood under the trees …'

Finn and Oliver knew something was wrong, stayed still and kept quiet.

We hurriedly started collecting branches.

'Let's tie them together,' I said, 'they'll make … well they'll spread the weight better!'

She dug in the kitbag, we'd brought orange twine, because you never know when you might need orange twine and we looped it round the middle of each branch and in five minutes we had enough to stretch out to the lamb.

Before she set off, I handed her the lead rope, 'tie this round your middle and if the bridge doesn't work Oliver can pull you out.'

'I'm going to lie down like I was swimming, that'll help me float on the surface, won't it?'

I agreed.

She looped the rope round her waist, knotted it and gave me the other end.

The ewe was getting really agitated. To add to its trouble the poor thing probably thought we were after its lamb.

Tulip lay down, carefully edged on to the branches and set off. My heart was in my mouth and I had a tight hold of the rope in case the bridge started to sink.

She crawled out, the branches rocked, swayed and sank a little.

'Uhh!', she stopped.

'TULIP!' I tightened my grip on the rope and got ready to pull her back.

She waited for a minute and then adjusted her position, 'I think it's okay.'

She set off again, the bridge didn't sink any more so she kept inching forward.

It only took seconds but it seemed like an age and the lamb was getting weaker. Just as it looked as if it was about to give up, Tulip reached it, slipped her hand under its head and raised it out of the mud. With her other hand she grabbed a handful of wool and pulled the lamb towards her.

'GOT IT!' she shouted triumphantly.

'Oliver,' I called. He carefully came closer, I tied the rope to his bridle, he waited until Tulip was facing the right way and turned. She held the rope in one hand and clutched the lamb tight in the other. Slowly Oliver walked away and pulled Tulip back.

The lamb was shivering, it was caked in mud but it looked fine. Tulip carried it towards its mother. The lamb saw her, wriggled frantically, jumped out of her grip and the two of them dashed away.

'Well don't say thank you,' Tulip called, as they disappeared into the trees.

'Baaaaa … ttttthhhhaaaank yyyouuu Ttttttuuuulip,' I said, pretending I was the mummy sheep. 'Yourrrr theeeee bbbbbest!'

'I probably deserve a reward,' she suggested.

'I'll make you a medal …' I offered.

'A chocolate one?'

'A fennel one …'

She pulled a face, 'I want a treat not a punishment.'

We pulled the makeshift bridge back and started unpicking the orange twine.

'Loreee …'

'Uh-huh!'

'I thought you had a store of chocolate to treat people who "done good"'

'Did you rescue the lamb because you wanted to save it or

because you wanted some chocolate?' I asked.

Tulip pretended to be outraged at the suggestion. 'I rescued him because I'm almost an angel.'

'I'll put it in the book and at the end of the trip we'll tot up your marks and see how you did …'

'You're the meanest person in this peat marsh Lori,' she complained.

'You did good, Tulip. Of course there is chocolate for you.'

'I could do with finding a stream first to wash my hands and can we give Oliver and Finn a carrot each as they did good too.'

Day 3
Chapter 4

'Got it sorted?' the receptionist asked as the two police officers returned to the station.

'Yeah, those lads had more luck on their side than they deserved,' said one.

'Specially Jonas Donnelly,' added the other.

The door opened and the duty sergeant came out.

'Thanks for keeping us in the loop, a bit more serious than anti-social behaviour then?'

'Kyle and Eddie are home now. Going to be suffering until the swellings go down, they've all suffered multiple stings but Jonas is being kept in. The doctors rushed him straight into intensive care. Severe anaphylactic reaction they say,' the first constable replied.

The sergeant sighed, 'how could they be so stupid, what possessed them to kick over bee hives?'

'Beats me sir …'

'Doesn't bear thinking about the potential consequences.'

'Yes sir, Doctor said another half an hour and there'd have been no coming back from the state Jonas was in.'

'Lucky kid,' the sergeant commented.

'Yes … if that girl hadn't phoned …'

'They owe her big time. And the other two? Do they realise the seriousness of the situation?'

'They do now sir. Kept our traps shut, let the doctors do

the talking and then drove them home. They were white as sheets, they asked if Jonas was okay and we just said he's in intensive care and left it at that.'

'Did you speak to their parents, Bryn?'

'Called Jonas's from the hospital and they were on their way when we left. Explained what's been going on to Kyle and Eddie's mums and dads when we took them back. Think they're going to keep a tight rein on them for a while. Sounds like Eddie was the ring leader so he's got some difficult weeks ahead of him; his mother looked less than pleased!'

'The papers know,' the sergeant said. 'Hugh Barlow contacted them. He's not a happy bunny. Wants the boys charged or compensation for kicking his hives over.'

'Not surprised.'

'A bit of nightmare for a beekeeper sir,' added the other constable. 'My uncle keeps bees and he's always banging on about how bees don't like being disturbed. Who would kick over a beehive anyway?'

The sergeant agreed, 'if I was going to do a bit of petty vandalism, it wouldn't be first on my list. They should have stuck to the traditional acts of teenage rebellion; knocking over bins, smashing windows or spraying rude words on walls, a lot less risky.'

The receptionist shuddered at the thought of bees, 'I run a mile if I see one and there's no way I'd go near a beehive - I'd need an anti-bee suit and one of them diver's helmets.'

'Do we know what the paper is going to say, Sir?'

'I imagine something about "teenage vandalism running

rife", "bring back the birch" and "send them off to join the army," ... maybe they'll be a bit softer on them when they find out how badly Jonas has been affected.'

'I'll write up my notes now ...'

The sergeant nodded, 'I'll give the parents a call, if they don't sort things out with Barlow, the kids will be charged.'

'What about the girl who called in, pretty charitable after the way they talked to her, sir?

'She doesn't have her mobile phone switched on, she's doing some trekking and her father gave it to her for emergencies. She did give us a home number so I'll phone when she's back, said she'd be there at the end of the week; I'll get the full story then.'

'Can't believe those boys would think it's okay to make comments like that to a fourteen-year-old! My son is twelve and he knows that's not right, he'd be embarrassed and appalled at the way they behaved!'

Day 3
Chapter 5

We found a stream, washed Tulip's shorts and top and let the horses drink.

While we waited for Tulip's clothes to dry, we played "Yes, No, Black, White". It was my turn first so I said are you ready? Automatically she said "yes" and I went 'that's one game to me!'

She went 'we haven't started, Lori' and we spent the next ten minutes arguing if that was fair.

I said, 'it was definitely fair …'

'No, it wasn't,' she claimed.

'Second game to me Tulip.'

She started laughing and said I was such a cheat.

'No, I'm not …'

'Third game to me …' she claimed triumphantly.

We decided to play the Minister's Cat instead.

The sun was so hot that after a couple of games her clothes were dry. We remounted, paddled through the water and carried on.

We rode on steadily, came to a forest on the side of a hill and weaved our way between the trees. When we eventually came out the other side, we found ourselves at the edge of a huge wild meadow.

The moment she saw it, Tulip jumped off Oliver's back with a wild cry of exultation. The wild flowers were so tall they reached her shoulders. 'This is the best place EVER!' she announced. 'Look at these they're so beautiful,' she picked a handful of blooms, 'WOW … they smell amazing!'

I got off Finn to see for myself, they were lovely, hints of sweet honey, fresh apple and surprisingly a very faint coconut aroma.

She picked some leaves.

'Ummm!' She tossed some to me, 'here you go Lorelei …'

I just managed to catch them as she rushed excitedly to the next plant and then the next.

'These are so good!' she squealed, 'tasty, tasty, tasty, the best I've ever had when I've been over.

We raced on, sampling different plants, while Finn and Oliver followed more sedately, munching on the fresh grass.

Tulip twirled round joyfully, ran into the middle of the meadow and suddenly the air was full of butterflies.

'OH WOW!' I gasped.

There were thousands and thousands, all different shapes, colours and sizes. They filled the air like a rainbow of petals. I stopped, stood as still as I could and after a few minutes they started to settle on me.

I turned slowly to Tulip, she was covered in butterflies too, she had her arms stretched out and they'd even perched on her finger tips.

'Come on, if you all work together …' she started.

The butterflies fluttered off.

'Oh … I was hoping they would lift me up so I could get a better view,' she grinned.

We walked on, butterflies flickered everywhere, even settling on the horses, who hardly noticed except for the occasional shake of their heads. The steady drone of bees was interspersed with the chirruping of grasshoppers, there were small ponds where shimmery dragonflies and damselflies hovered, darting everywhere to catch their lunch.

'Amazing,' said Tulip.

'What about all these bugs?' I asked.

'Yeah, it's a bit odd,' she agreed. 'You'd think birds would be here all the time for their dinner. Wait a minute, look over there!'

There were some taller trees to one side and when you squinted you could see nests in the highest branches.

'Hunting birds …' she said.

'There's loads of them, I thought they liked their own territory?' I said.

'They do, but perhaps these ones don't mind sharing, I mean there's plenty of space here,' suggested Tulip. 'Course like you tell me, "there are exceptions to every rule."'

A bird launched itself from one of the trees and headed south.

'He's massive,' I said, 'he must be an eagle.'

Tulip looked again, 'no, I think a goshawk, but a really big one, he's too grey for an eagle.'

Oliver snorted away a butterfly that had settled on his nose.

We wandered gleefully through the flowers, choosing some of the loveliest ones and putting them in each other's hair. Eventually we came to a small cliff. A waterfall was tumbling down the side and below it was a deep, crystal-clear pool. It was so hot we decided to cool down with a swim.

Finn and Oliver were quite content. The mooched about, nudging each other, one of them grazing while the other kept watch.

Eventually we climbed out and lay on the warm rocks at the side.

'You know Lori this is a perfect moment. I'm gonna lock it away in my head and if I'm ever sad or things are hard, I'll remember this and it'll make me happy.'

She was right. The sky was a deep blue, the sun was shining and the perfume of the wild flowers drifted over us. We lay there, in silence for ten minutes soaking it all in.

'Tulip?' I asked.

'Uh-huh?'

'Have you kissed a boy yet?'

'Course.'

'Who,' I asked.

'Trefoil …'

'You never have!' Trefoil was the boy every girl in her village fancied. He was older than her but everyone said he was sweet on Whitegowan.

'I have too!'

'Really … what was it like?'

'It was wonderful. It was like being in paradise,' Tulip said.

'Was it? What did you do?'

'We leant against each other and he kissed me, so gently …'

'And …' I wanted more details.

She giggled, 'you're jealous!'

'I'M NOT! I'm not jealous of him, he's far too pleased with himself. When?' I demanded.

'When we did the pageant. He was the Spring moon and I was the May sun …'

'HEY! That was years and years ago,' I complained. 'You were like six. I remember Moo,' that's what Tulip calls her mum, 'telling me about it.'

'I still kissed him and that's what you asked.'

'You know I meant a boy, a boy you might want as a boyfriend.'

'Have you kissed a boy then Lorelei?'

'No.'

'Why not?'

'I want to kiss a boy but I haven't found a boy I want to kiss yet. Hannah kissed one.'

'What was it like?'

'Disappointing. It was a boy called Lucas, he put his lips on hers and then sort of breathed. She thought he was going to put his tongue in her mouth, because she'd read that's what boys do.'

'Do they?'

'That's what she'd read. She stood there for twenty seconds and then as nothing else happened, she pulled away and said she was going to get some juice. She saw him later, he was talking to his mates and pointing to her and they were fist bumping him. She blanked him from then on. She said she and Kyla are going to practice together, because she's sure it's meant to be more fun than just someone breathing really close.'

'Trefoil just gave me a peck on the cheek, so I guess it wasn't a boyfriend kiss.'

'I suppose I should just wait until there's a boy I like enough to try out kissing.'

'There's plenty other things apart from boys …' Tulip pointed out. 'It'll happen when it happens.'

'You're so wise!'

'I know,' she added, 'beautiful, sweet and totally the cleverest person in this whole valley.'

'The second cleverest!' I corrected her.

'At least I'm not the wettest!'

'Aargh!'

Before I could roll out of the way she splashed me.

Oliver looked up at my scream and it was almost like he was saying behave yourselves.

We lay there for a bit longer while I dried off again.

Eventually it was time to get on, I was about to stand up, when Tulip gently touched my arm and pointed.

On the far side of the pool a Pine Marten snuck out of the long grass. It had a mouse in its jaws. It dropped the mouse, took a drink from the water, picked up its dinner and disappeared back into the long grass.

'He didn't hang around long …' I said.

'Bet he's worried about the Goshawk.'

'They'd hunt a Pine Marten?'

'Sure,' she confirmed. 'They're big birds, they eat rabbits, the Pine Marten is about the same size so why not?'

We were dry again, so we got dressed and got back on the horses.

'Do you think they can taste the difference between a rabbit and a Pine Marten,' I asked.

'I'd guess they're just glad to catch something,' she decided. 'It's not like they're going to be choosy, it's just going to be what they can find.'

'Yes but … if they're flying about and they see … I don't know a squirrel and a weasel do they go, "well I had squirrel for my tea yesterday, I think weasel would make a nice change"?'

'I think they go for whatever they think they're most likely to catch.' She thought about that for a moment, 'and also what's easiest and won't fight back. Maybe they prefer meat, but raiding a nest and eating eggs is much less hassle so sometimes they'll do that.'

'I suppose.'

'They want to waste as little energy as possible, I mean flying is hard work, that's why they glide as much as they can,' Tulip said.

'Yeah, I can imagine.' She's right of course, a sheep can stand in a field and eat all the grass he wants and he doesn't have to use up much energy. A bird has to find something to catch for his dinner each day, bugs or mice or rabbits and there's no guarantee; it's not like he can fly off to the nearest supermarket and flutter up and down the aisles picking out his favourites.

'Funny thing,' added Tulip, 'we eat rabbits and chickens and things that mostly eat vegetables but we don't eat things that eat meat, like weasels, or hawks do we?'

'I've never thought of that, I'll have to look it up when we get back.'

We were reluctant to leave the meadow, it was just so beautiful but we didn't want to leave it too late to arrive at Mr. and Mrs. Scott's house.

We set off again, made our way through a small wood and on the other side was an ancient drovers' road. The horses had had a drink, a good eat, a nice rest and they were ready for another gallop. We urged them on, pretending we were taking an urgent letter to the king of France. I'd told Tulip the story of D'Artagnan and the Three Musketeers and how they had to defend the kingdom from the wicked Count Richelieu and she'd liked it a lot. Actually I only knew about it from an ancient cartoon version, it was a bit mad because the musketeers were all talking dogs and so were all the other characters … well there might have been a talking bear in there somewhere! Dad had found it on line and made me watch it with him. It was pretty weird, these dogs were dressed up like people, walking like people and they even had hands not paws. They charged around the countryside doing heroic things but I can't think it was anything like the original book. Still, it gave me and Tulip an opportunity to wave pretend swords in the air and speak in French accents. Zut alors!

Oliver didn't want to be caught this time and when he gets going, he's a lot faster than Finn. Luckily before they got too far ahead, the path came to an end and they had to slow down.

'SACRE BLEU!' yelled Tulip triumphantly, 'the baguettes they are safe, we have rescued the cauliflowers and La France is again top mouse!'

Like I said I didn't have a very accurate starting point for my version and Tulip added even more nonsense.

Mr. and Mrs. Scott's house was only a couple of miles further on so we walked the last bit and made up more tales about the brave dog musketeers, their adventures and their thrilling schemes.

Day 3
Chapter 5

When Mrs. Lindsay gave us her friend's address, she warned us it was out on its own, a long way from the village. It really was, although it wasn't hard to find as there was just the one road. We knew we were there because out in the middle of the natural scrubland was a neatly trimmed hedge. We followed it until we came to a gate, I pressed the intercom and a lady said "hello" and "who is that?". I said who we were, there was a hum from a motor and the gate slid open. We trotted down the drive, the garden on either side wasn't much like a garden, there weren't any flowers just trees and bushes and they looked like they'd always been there. When we finally saw the house, it didn't really look like a house, just a massive stone wall, two stories high and really wide. There weren't any windows only a big door, nearer to one side than the other. A lady was standing in the doorway. She waved to us and came over.

'Mrs Scott,' I asked.

'Esme,' she said, 'welcome to Grey Stone House, girls.'

We introduced ourselves, I shook her hand and Tulip curtsied.

'This is ever so kind,' I said, 'are you sure it's okay?'

'Of course,' she said. 'I've been friends with Becca since Primary One, and when she was telling me about your trip, I insisted on helping out.' A man came out the front door, she turned and introduced him as her husband, Keir.

When Mr. Scott came closer he looked flustered, but pulled himself together and said hello. 'Yes,' he said, 'I'm Keir …'

'How do you do sir?' I said.

He breathed in deeply. 'Let me take you to the stables,' he offered.

'Thanks,' I said. 'Mrs. Lindsay said you have horses.'

'Keir's mad on horses,' his wife explained, 'that's why we live out here.'

Tulip asked if she liked horses too.

'I do ride,' she admitted, 'and I like being out on a horse but it's not my passion.'

Keir was making friends with Oliver and turned to his wife, 'you ride really well.'

'I spent plenty of time at Pony Club,' she admitted, 'but I was mainly there to meet boys!'

'Did you?' I asked.

'I met Keir so it worked out exactly as I'd hoped.'

'And did you go to Pony Club to meet girls, Mr. Scott?' asked Tulip.

'I went because of the horses; meeting Esme was the icing on the cake!'

'I'm in the middle of preparing dinner so I'd better get back to the kitchen,' Esme said. 'You go and sort out the horses.'

Mr Scott gave Finn a gentle stroke between his ears, 'look at you, you're already a star!'

Finn agreed with a whinny.

Mr. Scott led us round the building to the stable block.

'They're lovely animals,' he said, 'are they Becca's? They're in amazing condition …'

'Yes, they're Mrs. Lindsay's,' I agreed.

'They've been enjoying themselves, I think that's why they're looking good,' Tulip suggested.

He agreed and said they were really happy.

He led us to the stable block, which unlike the rest of the house was a proper old building.

'Mr. Scott …' started Tulip.

'Yes … you must call me Keir, Mr. Scott makes me sound like a school teacher or a bank manager.'

'Okey dokes, you know we don't mind you thinking we look wild.'

He went red.

'We're wild girls,' she added, 'but we're not bad or mad or dangerous.'

He cleared his throat. 'Was I that obvious? Esme warned me you'd be wild but I thought she meant you'd be like the teenagers you see on television, fourteen going on twenty-five. Glossy make-up, crop tops, you know trying to look like fashion models or pop stars. I hadn't appreciated she'd meant properly wild - that you could have come straight from a council of war with the ancient Celts and were ready to set about any Roman invader who dared cross the wall.'

'I'm always wild,' said Tulip, 'but Lori can look quite weird and boring, because that's how her school likes to see her. She's got a photograph of how she looks for her mum.'

I showed him my school photo.

He nodded his head and then said he thought I looked a lot better wild.

'You don't mind?' I asked.

'No, not at all. It just wasn't what I'd been expecting. Do you ride bareback all the time?'

'Yes,' said Tulip. 'Without the saddle Oliver can tell what I want him to do so it's a lot easier …'

'And always barefoot?'

'In summer, not so much when it gets cold,' I admitted.

He led us into the yard. There were six stables and he had two horses; a big white one and a smaller piebald.

'This is Archie,' he pointed to the piebald. 'The smartest horse I've had but he's getting on a bit so he's taking it easy and getting fat,' he explained with a laugh.

'And the white?' I asked.

'Maeve.'

'That's a very cool name,' decided Tulip.

'Let's put yours in these stalls,' he gestured to the two opposite his horses. 'It'll give the four of them a chance to check each other out and they won't be too close so Maeve and Archie shouldn't feel put upon.'

'Please, is there time to groom them and check for stones before we go in?' I asked.

'Of course, I'll give you a hand,' Mr. Scott said.

It didn't take long with the three of us and soon Finn and Oliver were gleaming. Mr. Scott fetched food for them and once they looked settled, we left them to it and he took us to the house.

It was quite different on the other side. Huge glass windows faced south and there was an amazing view.

'This is fantastic,' I said as we stood on the terrace.

'Totally,' agreed Tulip.

'We were going to build a traditional house but our architect suggested we should take the opportunity to see the view. He raised the house up and now when you're in the lounge, the kitchen or a bedroom you can see the landscape.'

We went inside and he took us to the bedroom we were sharing.

'Excuse me, would it be okay if we used your washing machine?' I asked. 'We've been washing, but it would be nice to give everything a proper clean.'

'Course.'

We took it in turn to have a quick freshen up, put on our big t-shirts and took our wearing clothes to their laundry.

Mrs. Scott was cooking so we gave her hand.

Mr. Scott was right the view from the kitchen was just as great as from the terrace.

Dinner was delicious. It's nice to have a proper meal every now and then.

'Has it been a good trip so far?' Mrs. Scott asked.

'Brilliant!' I said.

'Totally,' agreed Tulip. 'We've been extra lucky with the animals we've seen.' She went on to tell them about the badgers, the Pine Marten, the butterflies and the other creatures we passed. 'We rode right through a flock of sheep and they didn't bat an eye.'

'We met some more sheep later on and Tulip rescued a lamb from a swamp!' I said and told them the exciting details and how brave she was.

'You've been camping out but I didn't see a tent?' said Mr. Scott.

'We build shelters where ever we stop, it's easier than carting round lots of stuff,' Tulip said.

'Don't your mothers worry? Not just about living outside but there are some unpleasant people about?' asked Mrs. Scott.

'We've been staying away from villages and towns as much as we can,' I explained.

'Lori was shouted at by some stupid, mean boys but they just said nasty things and didn't chase after her,' said Tulip. 'We think they might have been drunk.'

'We have the horses; people don't mess with you when you're on top of big animal like Finn. Most folk don't understand horses so they're scared of them,' I added.

'That's true,' Mr. Scott agreed.

'It's fine out in the wild, at home I mostly live outside and I've been showing Lori,' explained Tulip.

'And Mum and Dad trust me now,' I added.

'You showed them didn't you, Lori?' said Tulip.

'Yes. I was nearly eleven when Tulip and I met and she taught me a bunch of stuff, you know about how to survive outdoors and how to know which way you should be going.

It was really lucky she did, because a couple of months later, me, Mum, Dad and Gus, he's my little brother, we got stuck in the middle of nowhere. There was a landslip, it took out the bit of road our car was on and we slid down into a valley like we were on a giant surf board. We were all okay but it would have been a tricky climb back up the hill and Dad decided we should walk down the dell to get help. We'd been going for a few miles when Dad slipped and hurt his leg. Gus was just a baby, so Mum couldn't leave him and Dad could hardly stand and definitely couldn't walk. Anyway I was the only one who knew where to go so I hiked thirty miles on my own to get help. After that Mum and Dad understood I knew what I was doing and that I was sensible.'

'Gosh,' said Mrs. Scott.

'I never just go off; I tell them so they know where I'm going and what I'm doing. And I have an emergency phone … well for emergencies.'

'At eleven! At that age I could just about be trusted to go into the garden on my own,' Mrs. Scott said.

Mr. Scott agreed, 'it was the same for me, not that I'd have survived further than a hundred metres from the biscuit tin!'

I pointed out I had an added incentive, 'I really did have to find someone to rescue Mum and Dad and Gus.'

'When you know what to do, it helps so much,' Tulip said.

We told them about all the things you can forage and how you can catch rabbits and fish and even birds and cook them.

'You can survive on plants and flowers but they don't

always give you everything you need so some meat helps,' explained Tulip.

In one of my classes there'd been a unit about nutrition so I added it would be okay if you could always find the right beans, nuts and grains, 'you need amino acids, stuff like that and in the wild, eating meat is the easiest way to get them.

'You two know your stuff,' said Mr. Scott.

'Makes us seem very boring, timid stay-at-home's,' Mrs. Scott added.

When we'd finished dinner, we helped wash-up and then we all sat in the sitting room to enjoy the view.

They asked where we'd been.

We showed them the route on their computer and told them about all the things we'd seen, like the chapel, the Reaney village and the big loch where we'd gone swimming.

Tulip remembered the half-finished house we'd passed, 'it looked like the saddest house on earth, do you know anything about it?'

'Whereabouts?' said Mr Scott.

I worked it out from our route.

'It's here, quite close to this town …'

'Someone had left flowers and toys and things like it was a grave,' explained Tulip.

Mr. Scott did a search, found a newspaper article and read it out to us.

No wonder we felt so glum when we were there, it was an awful story.

The people who owned it had lived in the town, they

had three children and their flat wasn't big enough so they decided to build their own house. They'd started the building and then went on holiday. Something went wrong with the boiler in the place they were staying and they were all poisoned while they were sleeping.

After the funeral, no one in the family wanted to finish the house, the builders stopped working because they weren't being paid and no one would buy it because they knew what had happened.

'According to the article their Gran and Granpa would visit to lay flowers and momentos,' Mr. Scott said, 'then the Gran died and the Granpa was even sadder and he moved away to get away from the memories.'

'Oh … how awful …' said Mrs. Scott.

Tulip and I agreed.

'We're always visiting old ruins,' said Tulip, 'but that was definitely the unhappiest place we've ever been.'

The four us sat in silence for a bit until Mr. Scott spotted deer in the field below the garden. A big stag, some younger ones and a few does were nibbling at the grass. That cheered us all up and the conversation moved on to the wildlife that lived around them and eventually it was time for bed.

Day 4
Chapter 1

The next morning, as usual Tulip and I were awake early. The horses were used to seeing us first thing and we decided to check they were okay. We didn't want to disturb Mr. and Mrs. Scott so we slipped out the back door, quietly like barn owls on the wing and tiptoed to the stables.

Finn and Oliver looked really happy. When they're happy horses smile, it's subtle but it's there. Their ears are perky, their lips sort of stick out and they half close their eyes. They were getting along fine with Mr. Scott's two horses, so we were pleased about that. We filled their feed bags, had a chat to them and then went across the yard to say hello to Archie and Maeve so they didn't feel left out.

Maeve was quite nervy and backed away. Tulip went to her stable door, stood silently looking up and Maeve calmed down. Archie wasn't at all shy, he came straight up to me to say hello and wanted a rub.

After a minute or so, curiosity got the better of Maeve, she came closer and Tulip was able to stroke her nose.

'That's better, she knows we're friends,' said Tulip

'She's only being nicer because she thinks you're a giant carrot.'

Tulip laughed and suggested it was because she was much taller than me so Maeve knew she was a real person and not a pixie.

'A PIXIE!!'

'Yes … a cute one, but very small …'

'I'm not small! And it's not like you're that much bigger!'

'I have to get things down from the top shelf in your house,' she claimed.

'That's only because you've got those weird extra-long arms.'

It was her turn to be outraged.

'I DO NOT, THEY'RE PERFECTLY NORMAL …'

'They're like the arms of an octopus!'

She thought about that for a moment. 'If I had eight arms that would be great, I could make bread, cook the dinner and beat you at "high-fives" at the same time!'

'Beat me? You can't beat me at high fives even when you're not doing anything else, you'd never beat me if you were trying to make bread too.'

'I can so! Right, I challenge you to "high-fives"!' Tulip dared me.

'I accept your challenge, get ready to eat humble pie!'

'It's you who'll be eating crow!' she retorted. 'Slap me five!'

At first we stood opposite each other trying to slap each other's palm. Then Tulip called, "down low!'

She pulled her hands away, 'TOO SLOW!' she yelled and ran off and I chased her.

Before we knew it, we were playing tig, which only stopped when we heard Mrs. Scott calling for us.

We raced each other back to the kitchen.

'Morning!' Tulip greeted her, 'HIGH FIVE!'

Mrs. Scott slapped her hand, 'down low …' and before Tulip could slap her hand she pulled it away, 'too SLOW!' she shouted and made Tulip giggle.

'Good morning,' I said pretending I was the sensible one.

'Been checking on the horses?'

'Yeah, we were up early and didn't want to wake you,' I said.

'They're good. Maeve, likes me better than she likes Lori!' claimed Tulip.

'Apparently Maeve prefers people who look like carrots …'

'Morning, morning,' Mr. Scott appeared. 'I have a fancy for bacon rolls, can I tempt the rest of you?'

We all agreed that would be perfect.

He got out the pan, cooked the bacon with a flourish while we buttered the rolls. After breakfast Mr. Scott asked if he could join us for the first part of the day.

'Of course … Mr. Sco … Keir,' I said.

Tulip was very cheeky, 'if you think you can keep up …'

'TULIP!' I reprimanded her.

'Gotta set the rules …'

'I'll come on Maeve then …' he decided.

Day 4
Chapter 2

We said goodbye and thank you to Mrs. Scott. She said to pass on her love to Becca when we saw her again.

Mr. Scott rode round the corner.

'I feel Maeve and I are over-dressed compared to you two, but I'm not used to riding without a saddle.'

'You look very smart, while we look … more casual … specially Tulip, who is so casual she looks like a scarecrow,' I said.

Tulip stuck her tongue out and then was straight up on Oliver. I adjusted my rucksack, mounted Finn and we set off.

I had the route in my head so I went first, then Mr. Scott and then Tulip. We got away from the road as soon as we could and made our way to the moors. After a mile we had a canter. Maeve was fast, but Mr. Scott was heavier than us and of course Finn and Oliver weren't carrying any extra weight like saddles or stirrups and all that stuff so we went gently on them.

He was really good though; much better than us. You could tell he'd been riding for a long time; everything he did was natural and easy.

When we were all back together, he asked how long we'd been riding for.

'Mrs. Lindsay started teaching us four years ago,' said Tulip.

'Only four years! She's done an amazing job.'

'I don't know, Oliver looks like he's got a sack of potatoes sitting on him!' I said.

'And poor Finn is carrying that little chest of drawers on his back,' Tulip countered.

He laughed, 'are you always so competitive?'

'We're not really, we just like arguing,' I admitted.

'You're both pretty good, you should try entering some competitions, I think you'd do well.'

I said I wasn't sure about that and explained I was already doing a lot of running for both my school and my club and didn't have much extra time to take up another sport, 'and Tulip's got plenty of work when she's home.'

'Yes,' Tulip agreed, 'I like riding for the fun of riding, I don't think I'd like it so much if I knew people were marking me. And actually, I don't know that we're all that good. Oliver and I work well together but I don't think I'm anywhere near so good when I'm on Finn and I bet it'd take me an absolute age to persuade Maeve to do what I wanted.'

Tulip's quite wise … well sometimes.

Mr. Scott considered what she'd said for a moment. 'I think that's because you're still really beginners in a way. There are lots of little things that you can only learn through experience.'

'I like the running races, especially the winning,' I admitted, 'but that's just up to me. If I push myself the only one who suffers is me, it'd be a bit different if I was responsible for a horse too.'

He agreed, 'I loved competing but it's not for everyone.'

We were thinking about that when he changed the subject. 'Last night you said you like exploring ruins, there's an interesting old building not too far off the path.'

'That would be cool, Kier,' I said.

Tulip asked him about the competitions. 'Were you any good?'

She's not shy about asking things like that.

He was happy to tell us about it. He'd won a lot of big competitions, his ambition had been to ride in the Olympics, 'but when it came to the trials, I came to see I just wasn't good enough,' he admitted.

'You seem pretty amazing to me,' Tulip offered.

'I had a great horse, a brilliant coach but in the end no matter how hard I worked I just couldn't beat the very top people. They had all the skills and then something else. A natural understanding, I guess, Finn and Lori have it and you and Oliver, but the top people could get on any horse and it was like they'd always been together.'

'Do you miss competing?' I asked.

'It was awful when I stopped, I felt like a failure.' He shrugged his shoulders, 'Esme coaxed me out of my disappointment, she showed me I could channel my competitive energy into something else. I went into business and discovered the ability to analyse and solve problems when I was competing, transferred to building up companies. It's not quite the same thrill as a clear show-jumping round or being the fastest on the cross-country course but it pays a lot better and it means I get to ride for fun.

We chatted away until he pointed out a path. 'The building is just along there.'

We trotted down the hill until we came to a river and Mr Scott led us upstream to a big stone house. Trees had grown around it but deer or sheep or rabbits must have been coming because the grass in front had been cropped so it looked a bit like a lawn

'It's an old mill!' exclaimed Tulip.

It just looked like a ruin to me. Don't get me wrong it was lovely, a wild briar was growing up the side, the flowers were in bloom and they smelt great but I couldn't tell it was anything more than just an old house.

'What a wonderful place. It's a shame it's not working any more,' she added.

'It's a bit too far from the village. After they invented steam engines, they didn't need water to drive the millwheel any more so they could put mills anywhere' Mr. Scott explained

Tulip was off Oliver in a flash, clambering over the broken door and heading inside to explore.

I checked with Mr. Scott, 'is it safe?'

'It's not going to fall down but watch out there may be rotten floorboards,' he warned.

That didn't sound too bad so I slipped off Finn and cautiously followed Tulip in.

The waterwheel was still there but the millrace had been blocked further up with a big sheet of iron. There was large pond above the building and water was spouting through a narrow channel, frothing and churning below us.

It was just an old building now, nothing was going to work again but some of the machinery was still there. Enormous iron cogwheels, spindles and the big, round milling stones.

Tulip was studying the mechanism.

'Isn't this place amazing? It must have been pretty special …'

'Why?' I asked.

'In a simple one they'd have had the one stone and they'd only be able to use the mill when there was a ton of water coming down. Here they could switch to one of these smaller stones,' she gestured, 'and keep on working even when the stream was low.'

'Oh …'

She pointed to a lever. 'It's jammed up now but that's how they switched from the biggest mill stone to one of the others.'

'I've always wondered about that,' said Mr. Scott. 'I'd thought it was so they could grind the flour into different sizes.'

Mr. Scott wandered up stream to look at the mill pond.

Tulip pointed out the bits of the mechanism to me and explained how the mill worked.

'The wheat would have come in here,' she gestured, 'and then they'd have stored it up in the top,' she pointed to a trap door above us.

'Must have been some slog, carrying sacks all the way up

there,' I suggested.

'They used a water powered pulley to ...'

Mr. Scott was bending over, suddenly he yelled, in a split-second Tulip disappeared and reappeared beside him thinking he was going to fall in. She was about to grab him when he pulled something out of the water and stood up.

'What about this?' he said.

She looked back to me in horror, worried she'd given herself away.

He turned round. 'Oh, there you are, hadn't realised you were right behind me, I didn't mean to shout.'

'It's fine,' I said quickly.

'Look at this little beauty, do you know what he is?'

I breathed a silent sigh of relief. It was okay, he hadn't seen her do her thing.

He was holding an ugly little creature with big pincers.

'Look at the size of those claws,' I said

'It's a crayfish,' Tulip said.

'That's right,' Mr. Scott agreed.

'Crayfish? He looks like a giant bug, can I see?' I asked.

'Watch he doesn't nip you,' said Mr Scott.

'Hold him behind the head,' advised Tulip.

I did as she said. 'He's looks fierce, is he poisonous?'

'No, he's like a lobster. Quite tasty people say, not that I've ever eaten one,' said Mr. Scott.

'They're okay if there's nothing better ...' decided Tulip.

'Are there more?'

'Yes, you can seen them down there Lori,' he pointed to

the side of the mill gate.'

There were more of the creatures and plenty of fish too.

'People don't come here,' Mr Scott explained, 'so nature has been allowed to get on and do its own thing.'

'Quite right,' I said and gently slipped the crayfish back into the water. It stayed where it was for a moment and then scooted off backwards.

'I only found this place by chance,' he explained. 'I was out for a ride, the rain started and I saw the trees from the trail. I thought I'd find shelter in the woods until the worst was past. The downpour was heavier and longer than I expected so it was a godsend finding a building with a roof. I did wonder about buying and rebuilding it and then I decided it was nicer knowing this bit of history was close by and nobody knew about it.'

'Yeah,' I agreed.

'Lots of animals use this place, deer, foxes, otters so they'd have all had to find somewhere else to live too,' added Tulip. 'I'm going to have a look at the view!'

We followed her up the steps. It was stone building, the roof was made from large, heavy slates and the windows were tiny so it had stayed dry inside and there was little rot.

From the top floor we could see for miles.

Mr. Scott pointed west, 'you're heading that way, aren't you?'

'We've almost reached our turning back point,' I said. 'We'll find somewhere to camp tonight then we'll be on our way home.'

'No map?'

'I've a pretty good memory,' I explained.

'But how on earth do you know which direction you're going?' he asked.

Tulip explained, 'we use the sun mainly but there are lots of other things, flowers, trees and moss that can help you work out north and south.'

'It's like being out with the junior SAS,' he laughed.

'Mounted division,' I said, then realised Tulip was about to ask what the SAS was and since most people over here know that sort of thing, I quickly got her to explain how we used the sun to find north.

Mr. Scott was fascinated and took out his phone to make notes. 'That's so sensible, I wish someone had explained it to me when I was younger. All those wasted hours I spent trying to work out how to get home. Annoyingly it's probably time for me to head back now.'

'Maybe we could meet you for a longer ride sometime,' I suggested.

'That would be fun … so long I don't have to forage for my dinner. Unlike you I don't think I'd survive on what I could find! You don't come across many jam doughnuts in the wild!'

'You could bring a bag of doughnuts,' said Tulip, 'a sharing bag,' she added.

'Thank you for letting us stay, we've had a lovely time and it was great to meet you and Mrs. Scott.'

'You've got our phone number …'

'Uh-huh!'

'If you need help you just call us, if it's an emergency we're a lot closer than your families.

'Thank you,' I said.

Day 4
Chapter 3

Tulip and I remounted, waved goodbye and rode off. When we were out of hearing, Tulip said she thought Mr. Scott was a bit sad. 'He wanted to come along …'

I agreed, 'but you know it's not because he wants to be with us in particular, it's more the freedom we have. We don't have responsibilities like he does, we can just go places and do what we want.'

'But this is a holiday for us, when we're back we'll have lots of things to do.'

'Yes, but look at us from his point of view, we're not carting about luggage, we can find food where we want and we're not tied down. I bet he's got an important job and he has to think about it a lot. He's seeing us and he's seeing what it's like to be a kid again.'

'S'pose, but we have things to worry about too …'

'Sure, but they're littler things aren't they?' I said. 'Anyway he was nice and so was Mrs. Scott.'

'They were lovely, but aren't we here to ride?'

'Yes …'

'SO!'

In flash Oliver was away, they'd caught us napping and we chased after them; already way, way behind.

The sun was shining, the wind was blowing through my hair and it was like being in Dad's open topped sports car.

Finn was skimming over the ground moving so smoothly it was like flying. Ahead Tulip was yelling excitedly urging Oliver to go faster.

It felt wonderful and we only stopped when we came to a river. It looked too deep and fast-flowing to cross but it was a good time to call a halt anyway. We dismounted, let the horses drink, gave them some food and set up the salt lick.

'Where now, Lori?' asked Tulip

'The bridge is upstream, there's an old road on the other side and we can follow it round that big forest.'

She examined it for a moment. 'Hey Lori, we should go through the middle; it'd be more exciting.'

'Would it?'

'Yes, it's a magic wood,' she said.

'How do you mean?'

'Look at those trees, they're not like normal trees, they can walk and talk,' she claimed.

'Like people?'

'Like big, wise people,' she said. 'They're snoozing now but if you're a bad person, like the mushroom man or that hoity toity woman, they'll wake up and trap you inside. They'll keep showing you new paths but you'll never find the one that leads out.'

'They're asleep now?' I asked.

'Sure, it's the middle of the day so they're doing that thing you said they do in Spain.'

'Siesta?'

'That's it. They've been busy all morning, they've had some

lunch and now they're having a doze. However … they're really light sleepers and if anyone so much as steps in they'll wake up,' Tulip explained.

'And …?' I asked.

'They'll see if you're good or a bad person.'

'Will they, how?'

'Often they just know but sometimes they're not completely sure so they have to work it out.'

'How do they do that?' I asked.

'They push their roots real close to the surface, so when anyone walks by just like Oliver knows how I'm feeling and what I want to do, so do the trees.'

'They must be super sensitive.'

'They are. If you're selfish or greedy or if you're like those stupid boys and hurt people's feelings for fun and don't care if you upset people they'll quickly find out,' Tulip said.

'What then?'

'Once they know who the bad ones are Lori … well …' she shook her head.

'What?'

'They keep them in the forest …'

'Do they? For how long?'

'Probably forever; their clothes will get ragged, their shoes will fall apart and they'll grow big beards,'

'Even the girls?'

'Of course not the girls!'

'Just checking …'

'To be precise then, smarty pants, "the boys" will grow big

bristly beards, "the girls" will get hairy ears and everyone's fingernails will become long and twisty like willow branches in winter.'

'What about their families, their mums and dads, or their wives or husbands, they're going to miss them.'

'Well, they should have thought about that and not been such rotten toads.'

There was a moment of silence, and then she added, 'sometimes if they work hard on being better people, the trees might let them out.'

'Good, there's got to be a chance to redeem yourself …' I said.

'But if they shout rude words or try and bash their way out, the trees will get angry. They won't let the really nasty ones out ever; when those people lie down, knobbly roots will push out of the ground so they can't sleep, wherever they walk sharp flints will stick into their feet and brambles will jab their skin and they'll never, ever get comfortable,' said Tulip.

'Sounds pretty dicey.'

'Through the forest is the quickest way so we've got to risk it,' she looked behind us, 'there are wolves on our heels and we'll never get away from their snapping teeth if we go the long way round the outside!'

'Wolves! In that case it'd be safest to go through the forest.'

'The lesser of two weevils,' Tulip agreed.

'It's lucky I'm a naturally good and helpful person so I'll

look after you. Stay close and you won't get tricked into getting lost,' I said.

'ME!'

'Yes you, little Miss Trouble …' I agreed.

'You're the one who's gotta be careful! I'm the nicest, kindest girl ever!' she claimed.

We walked along the river bank to the bridge, the grass looked good so we let Finn and Oliver take their time and graze as they went.

The bridge was quite new with a well-worn path leading to it.

'Plenty of people walk here,' said Tulip.

'Over that way there's a town,' I pointed to the right, 'I guess they come here to walk their dogs and stuff.'

'We're not camping here?'

'No, I've found a place well away from any roads or paths and according to the map there's an old fort on top of a near-bye hill. Once we get past the town it'll be another ten miles.'

Finn and Oliver were ready to get on, we mounted, crossed the bridge and followed the path into the wood. Moss had grown over everything, the ground, the fallen trees and even the rocky outcrops. Bracken, lush and green, was growing in the dappled patches of sunlight between the trees. It was like walking through a huge painting, the ground was soft and springy like it was made of foam and it felt so peaceful.

I said to Tulip we must have passed the test because the path stayed the same and she said I should be thankful she had such a sweet nature.

I said 'of course' and 'thank you'.

She ignored my sarcasm, she'd spotted something and instead pointed above us. 'Look!'

It was a nest.

'That's big, what sort of bird built that,' I asked.

She whispered to Oliver to stop and then climbed on his back to see if she could get a better view.

'Look at all the leaves, I think it might be a "drey",' she said.

'What's that?'

'A squirrel's nest …

Someone called to us, 'hello there, hello!'

A lady was walking up the trail. She was in paint-splattered dungarees, her hair was tied back in a headscarf and she had a small notebook with her.

'Are your horses okay with people?' she asked.

'Hi,' I said. 'Yes, they're very gentle.' I turned Finn round so he could see where the voice was coming from.

'I read somewhere you should always talk if you meet a horse and let them know you're there and then they don't get panicked and defensive. I thought it sounded a sensible plan, so that's why I called,' the lady said.

'That's right,' said Tulip. 'You don't like surprises, do you Oliver?'

Oliver flicked away some flies.

'Now they know you're here they'll be fine,' I agreed.

'Have you found something interesting?' she asked when

she was closer.

'It's a nest we think it might be a squirrel's,' I said.

'Interested in nature?

'Yes, it's wonderful, everywhere you go you see something different,' Tulip explained.

I slipped off Finn's back and added that we loved exploring, 'rootling out new places, forests, valleys, rivers and lakes and if we find any old ruins that's just the best.'

'You're not from round here?'

I guess I've never lost my accent, even though we've been living in Scotland for four years. 'We live near Edinburgh but I was born in Barnes.' I put on a cockney accent, 'I'm a Londoner, would you Adam and Eve it?'

She laughed.

'We're spending a week, the two of us, doing some horse packing. Basically it's a chance to wander a friend lent us her horses so we've come a lot further than usual.'

'It's been a fantastic trip,' said Tulip, who jumped off Oliver and came over to join the conversation.

'Do you live here miss?' I asked the lady.

'I'm up for the summer. I'm a painter, I'm working on some pieces for a show in the autumn and I needed a break from the studio. It's so lovely in the forest, I like to get out for an hour or so and then I'm completely refreshed when I go back.'

'Do people pay you for painting pictures?' Tulip asked.

'Yes, that's how I make my living ...'

'Wow, that is totally incredible.'

We walked along with her and she told us about her paintings.

We reached the path that led to her home and she was about to say goodbye when she saw the rings on Tulip's fingers.

'Those are extraordinary,' she remarked.

Tulip held her hand up and studied them. 'You know they're so much part of me I don't really think about them, they are nice aren't they?'

'Can I have a closer look?'

Tulip held out her hand, the lady touched her finger and a look of pain crossed Tulip's face.

'Miss?'

'Uh-huh …' she was studying the rings.

Tulip caught my eye and nodded so I knew to back her up.

'Miss, you need to speak to a doctor, I think he needs to do some tests on you … I don't think you're well.'

'What do mean?' the lady asked.

'I think it's urgent,' Tulip gave me a look.

'Properly urgent?' I asked.

'Yes,' said Tulip. 'Like you should see someone super quick.'

'Really?' I checked to be sure, 'super quick?'

'Uh-huh,' Tulip agreed.

'Okay, I'll call an ambulance …' I dug my phone out and turned it on.

'WHAT? NO … no I'm fine,' the lady protested.

Tulip was staring at her head and touched her lightly just above her ear and winced. 'You're not, you MUST see a doctor,' she insisted.

If Tulip ever says anything about people being ill, I never question her because she's always right, I mean there was that time when Gus had the virus when he was a baby and two years ago she knew something was wrong with Mum's tummy and made Dad take her to the hospital. The nurse took Mum away to examine her and before Dad knew it, she'd been whisked into the operating room and her appendix was out. She hadn't had any pain and she hadn't even felt poorly.

'Okay,' I dialled, I said to the man there was an emergency and told them where we were. They said they'd be there as quick as they could. They asked me what the problem was.

'The problem?' I asked Tulip.

'It's like in her head there's a special pipe and it's about to break …'

I repeated it to the ambulance man.

The lady protested, 'girls you shouldn't be playing games, calling out an ambulance is a waste of their time. There is no place for pranks …'

'The ambulance people say they'll be no more than ten minutes,' I said.

'This is ridiculous, I'm perfectly well …' she snapped. 'I'm going home …'

She turned but she couldn't go anywhere because Finn had come up to see what the hold-up was.

'Miss, you have to trust my friend. It's not a prank. At least you can see what the ambulance men say …' I told her.

Tulip nodded, 'I can tell miss, honestly. There's something wrong, they'll be able to tell you what it is exactly and they can give you the right medicine.'

'We should go to the road and meet them,' I suggested.

She was cross but since the ambulance was on its way, she reluctantly agreed to come and we walked in silence until we were out of the forest.

We were hardly there when the ambulance appeared. Two lady paramedics got out and asked where the patient was.

'I'm really sorry …' the lady started. 'I don't know what prompted these girls to call you, I'm perfectly fine.'

'There's something not right, like there's a sort of road way in her head and it's getting all jammed up,' said Tulip.

'The notes say a pipe in the head, do you mean an aneurysm?' the younger paramedic asked.

'I don't know,' admitted Tulip. 'What's an aneurysm?'

'It's when one of the tubes carrying blood around the brain bursts.'

'YES, yes it must be that …'

The lady interrupted, 'look there's nothing wrong with me, I don't have a headache, my vision is good and I've just been for a brisk walk …'

'Well …' the paramedic looked like she was going to give the lady the benefit of the doubt.

'We don't want you to waste the hospital's money,' I said. 'Mum gave me some emergency cash. This is an emergency, you can have it to pay for the petrol, for your time and if there's any left-over maybe pay for some testing,' I said. I dug out the money mum and Mr. Lindsay had given us and held it out to them. 'I'm sorry but this is all we have …'

The older paramedic smiled. 'No, no, you don't need to pay for an ambulance so just put it back.' She turned to the lady, 'These two girls are pretty convinced so perhaps you should at least come for some tests miss.'

'Really this is too much!'

'Better safe than sorry,' the younger one agreed. 'It pays to listen to people, perhaps this young lady has had some premonition or maybe she can tell, some people can. Anyway, we're here now, the hospital is only thirty minutes away. We can take you there, you'll have a scan and be back home in a couple of hours. If nothing's wrong, you won't have wasted much time but if an aneurysm is ticking away, it'd be best to find out soonest.'

The lady sighed and got in the back of the ambulance. 'Okay, I'm really sorry if this turns out to be a waste of time.' She paused for a moment … 'thank you girls I guess you're doing what you think best.'

'Good luck miss,' I said as the doors shut.

We watched the ambulance drive off.

'I hope she's okay,' I said.

'I hope so too, the thing in her head really needs to be sorted,' said Tulip.

'Or?'

'We should think of happier things,' she decided, 'thanks

for listening to me when I make you do these mad things like calling up ambulances and staying away from some places.'
    'Tulip, I trust you.'

Day 4
Chapter 4

We took the path that headed away from the town and pretty soon we were back in the wilderness. It was a bit of a ride to the next stop so we didn't do too much talking and concentrated on getting there.

When we arrived at the forest, we rode deep into it looking for a good spot. There was a big, old beech tree standing on its own with an apron of grass around it. The roots had grown out of the ground so there was a space underneath them. We sorted out the horses and then collected sticks, built a wall at the front, plastered it with mud and when we'd finished you could hardly tell there was a gap behind.

We foraged for our tea, then as a treat we had a Chocolate Freddo each and as it was still light, we decided to go for a walk.

'You said there's a fort?' asked Tulip

'On the map it said it's prehistoric, I don't think there can be much left now,' I said.

'Let's have a look.'

'If nothing else it's on the top of a hill so there should be a good view,' I said.

'We'll need to be careful,' decided Tulip with a serious look.

'Raiders?'

'Uh-huh,' she agreed, 'and they'll try to ambush us.'

We crept up the slope checking for enemy patrols. Was that a glint of metal? Were those figures in the shadows? Was that rasp the sound of a leather harness? We kept low, moved slowly and snuck up to the front gate.

Sheep had been grazing the area so we could see the walls quite clearly, the fort covered the whole of the top of the hill, there were three rings of ramparts and then a big flat area at the top.

We walked round the whole of the inner wall, the villagers had chosen a perfect spot with views every which-way; they would have easily spotted if any of their enemies tried to sneak up. It must have been a pretty important sort of place as it was so huge. We pretended everything was still there, the big huts where they gathered to meet, the smaller buildings where they did their trading with other villages and the little cottages where they lived. We wandered about, chatted to each other in an old-fashioned way as if we were the villagers.

'Forsooth how goes the harvest, good sir,' I said aloud.

'It is a good crop, the winter stores shall be full ere the month is out,' Tulip replied. 'And what is the news from the battlefield?'.

'We have been victorious, soon we shall celebrate and there shall be dancing, songs and feasting, yum-yum,' I said.

'Yum-yum?' she repeated askance.

'Totally,' I agreed and made her laugh.

We dodged the scruffy, almost wild dogs who would have been scavenging and poking their noses into everything.

'Verily, what an odour,' I said.

We held our noses.

It would have been extra smelly; the animals would have lived in the village, horses, cows, sheep, chickens, ducks, geese and pigs, some for food and some for bartering. They kept them close to stop people stealing them.

It would have been pretty full on. The people who lived here would have been busy, busy, busy in their cottages, cooking food, making pots or sewing clothes and we admired their skill and said "how fair" their work was. There would have been blacksmiths forging farming tools and of course swords, spears and knives since they would have needed to defend themselves. Not everyone would have been making things, there would have been story tellers and poets and musicians too. The place would have been buzzing, as night approached, Tulip pretended she was the chief and sent everyone, except the sentries, to bed and that meant it was nice and quiet.

We lay down to watch the sun setting.

The sky went from a pale orange to an amazing deep red … then as we were waiting for the sun to dip under the horizon, a lorry drove up one of the rough tracks below us.

'It's a bit late for fetching sheep, isn't it?' suggested Tulip.

The driver and his friend got out. They had dogs and started to round up the sheep.

'Those dogs are pretty good,' I said.

Tulip agreed. 'They've done this loads of times.'

We watched because it's always cool to see people do

things well, then we both had a bad feeling. It didn't seem right, the men kept looking around as if they were checking to see if they were being watched.

'They look shifty, don't they?' said Tulip.

'Yeah,' I agreed.

'It's really late to be moving animals about,' she added.

We watched for a bit longer.

'They're stealing them,' decided Tulip.

'You think?' I said.

'You shouldn't take other people's stuff, the trees would definitely never let you go if you did that,' said Tulip.

'But they might just be going about their business? Like they're collecting them to take to market in the morning?'

'Those lambs are too small for market ...' Tulip pointed out.

'Maybe they're taking them to the farm to feed them or so they can put them through the sheep dip tomorrow.'

'No. Why would they do it in the dark, they've had all day? They're definitely stealing them!'

We stared down at the men, who were hurrying now.

'Stealing is so bad,' she was roused now.

'What if you're wrong, the farmer might not like us poking our noses in ...' I warned.

'I'm right, let's get the horses and stop them ourselves,' Tulip said.

'WHAT? We will not be doing that!' I said firmly.

One of the men came back to open the back door and lower the ramp so they could load the sheep into the lorry. I had to make a decision or Tulip would be off to sort out the men on her own and that could cause plenty of trouble.

'Come on, we could sort them out,' she wheedled.

'NO! That is so not what we're doing! But what if the farmer shouts at us for bothering him this late?'

'Okay we go to the farmer and say your sheep are being stolen,' she decided, 'if he's says no they're not and gets cross then we just say sorry for being pests … but if they are stealing sheep he needs to know.'

'Well okay.'

We hurried back, collected Finn and Oliver and cantered across the fields to the nearest farm.

'I don't suppose five minutes of them being angry is too bad,' I admitted.

'If they are angry when all we're doing is trying to help then I'll give them a proper telling off for being ungrateful,' she said.

When we got there, I decided it would be better all-round if Tulip stayed with the horses and I went up on my own and knocked on the front door.

'Yes? What do you want?' the man who came out, looked me up and down and was very sharp. 'Who are you?'

I stepped back nervously and told him how we'd been at the top of the hill fort and saw men rounding up sheep. 'It's real late, we thought we should say but … but if they're meant to be fetching them …'

He shook his head as if to clear it.

'If they're meant to be doing it … well … well I'm sorry

we've disturbed you,' I added.

'You saw people rounding up sheep?'

'They had a big lorry,' and I explained how we'd seen them coming up the road from the south.

'Those damn thieves, back again!' he growled.

He pulled out his phone. He called the police first, then phoned some other people and told them what was happening. He said to get the tractors out and then said the names of some roads.

He yelled to someone inside. 'Those bastards are taking sheep from the Eilde Moor, but we've got them this time.'

'Thanks lass,' he said as he ran to the barn.

He reappeared on a four-wheel drive buggy and headed in the direction where the thieves had stopped their lorry.

A lady came to the door. 'Don't do anything stupid,' she shouted to the farmer, then turned to me, 'did he call the police?'

'Yes ma'am. Did we do wrong, we just thought you should know.'

She softened, 'no you did right. I'm sorry I sounded snappy I was just worried he'd set off half-cocked on his own.'

'He phoned the police Miss, and he phoned some other people and said to block roads with their tractors …'

'Good, good. You saw the thieves?'

'Yes Miss, well just from a distance. We were watching the sun set when we saw a lorry drive up…'

'A lot of them?'

'Two Miss …'

Her phone rang and I moved away so she didn't think I was eavesdropping.

I waited for a minute but we'd done our bit, there wasn't anything more to tell her so I went back to Tulip, mounted Finn and we set off back to our camp.

'He looked raging when he left. What's he's going to do? Are we in trouble?' Tulip asked.

'No, we're not in trouble, the lady said we did good.'

'There, told you,' she said, smugly.

'You're so smart. The farmer called the police first and then told his friends to block the roads. He swore! He said "DAMN", and "BASTARDS," so yes, you were right. I think they're planning to block the roads before the thieves can drive away with the sheep, then the police can come and arrest them and put them in prison.'

'I hope they don't start fighting with each other … although the pixies would love that,' she said.

'Would they?'

'For sure, pixies are always squabbling amongst themselves and they really like to goad someone else to fight and then they can watch.'

'That's not nice …'

She shrugged, 'I think they like the entertainment.'

It was dark by the time we got back to camp; we could see lights in the distance but we couldn't see what was happening. The sound of tractor engines echoed in the valley and then as we were about to go to bed, flashing blue lights lit up the sky.

'What's that?' Tulip asked.

'The policemen's car. I think that's the end of the sheep stealing for those people for a while.'

'Good, like I said, stealing is wrong,' said Tulip.

Day 5
Chapter 1

When we got up in the morning it was misty and real chilly so we ran about waving our arms in the air to get warm. Finn and Oliver watched us dashing around and you could tell they thought we were quite mad.

Tulip foraged for our breakfast while I sorted the horses. Something caught her eye and she squatted down to have a closer look.

'HEY!'

'What have you found Tulip?'

'Hoof prints, deer were here last night.'

'Cool, they weren't bothered by the horses then?'

'They don't eat the same things as Oliver and Finn, so it's not like they're competing,' she explained, 'but they didn't come too close'.

I crouched beside her and inspected the ground; they must have been grazing the bushes.

'Roe deer,' said Tulip.

'Really?'

'Uh-huh, see the shape and size of the prints,' and explained how they were different from other deer.

'They were so near, ooh I wish I'd been awake to see them,' I complained.

'They probably ran away at that snoring of yours!' she said.

'MINE!"

'They heard you and thought the big sheep lorry was about to drive through here,' Tulip said.

'I do not sound like a lorry, anyway like I told you I don't snore!'

She made a loud snorting sound.

Oliver heard her and snorted back.

'Even Oliver agrees! It was just like that!'

'What a lie!' I said.

'You should sleep in the vegetable patch then your snoring could frighten off the pigeons!' she continued.

I threatened her with a tickling and she ran to the other side of the big oak.

'It's so loud you could frighten off lions and tigers too,' she added.

I faked to go left round the trunk and then sprinted the other way. I'd fooled her, she gave a yelp when she realised, raced up the slope but her foot slipped and I managed to catch her. I was about to tickle her when the sun started to burn through the mist.

'Hey! We'll get a great view from the fort, let's get sorted and get up there before we leave,' I said.

It only took a couple of minutes to empty the grass out of the cotton bags, collect the salt lick and make sure we left everything as we'd found it. We mounted and trotted up to the top of the hill.

We arrived just in time. The countryside below was smothered in fog, but as we watched, it started to lift. Slowly the hills appeared, then the tops of the taller trees and soon the fields, hedges and a solitary house emerged. The mist hung around the valleys and around the rivers so it was like a painting.

We stayed for ages it was so beautiful, we were about to leave when we heard a motor. For a moment I thought it might be more people stealing sheep but it was the farmer's buggy. A trail led to the bottom of the fort, he drove up as far as he could, stopped and got off.

He waved and shouted, 'HEY … HEY GIRLS …'

He looked friendly and we rode down to meet him … but we didn't dismount just in case.

Day 5
Chapter 2

'I hoped you'd still be here …' he said, when we got close.

'We didn't take anything, we didn't even light a fire, honestly …' I hurriedly assured him.

'No, no you're not in trouble, I wanted to thank you,' he replied. 'You'd gone before I had a chance.'

'I didn't want to eavesdrop on your wife while she was on the phone,' I explained, '… it might have been a private call.'

'We're really grateful, all of us who farm round here,' he said. 'Those bar…' he managed to catch himself in time, 'err … those gentlemen have been stealing sheep from round here for a while now and nobody has been able to spot them. Thanks to you that's them nabbed. They won't be taking our stock for some time to come.'

'Good,' said Tulip, 'them cuckoos are bad.'

'You're right Miss … ,' he agreed, turned to her, his eyes flickered and he stuttered to a stop, 'c-c-cuckoos,' he finally said.

'We're glad you caught them,' I said.

He forced himself to stop staring at Tulip and turned to me. 'I've been speaking to some of the local farmers, we'd like to give you a reward, to thank you for being aware and for letting us know.'

'We don't need a reward, we didn't really do anything, we just came down and said to you.'

'You didn't even have to do that, so there's got to be something …' he said.

'Honestly we don't need anything,' I said.

'Chocolate,' interrupted Tulip.

'Of course,' said the farmer.

What is she like? So I added, 'well … a coffee would be nice.'

'And some feed for the horses,' Tulip suggested.

'Come down to the farm and I'm sure we could sort that,' he said.

We followed him to his house and his wife was waiting at the front door

'I'm Ben by the way,' he said, 'and this is my wife, Morna. Morna I've brought back the two girls who saved our flock,' he said.

'Thank you, thank you …' she said.

'We didn't really do anything …' I said.

'You did everything,' said Mr. Ben.

'And who are you, Miss …?' Morna asked.

'I-I-I,' I stuttered I couldn't think of an excuse not to say our names but if I did, they'd remember Tulip and we didn't want that.

'Coffee and breakfast,' the farmer said quickly, 'and some chocolate?'

'Thanks, coffee would be great,' I said. 'We've already had breakfast …'

'You brought it with you,' his wife asked.

'We foraged,' explained Tulip. 'There are plenty of berries

and fruit about.'

'Gosh, you're quite the wild girls,' she commented and then headed to the kitchen.

The farmer waited until his wife disappeared and beckoned us closer. 'My family have been here so far back no one knows when they first arrived,' he said 'and I've lived with the land all my life. I've learnt plenty, been taught plenty and seen plenty.'

'You have?' I asked.

He nodded and then mostly looking at Tulip, he said, 'I understand about names, keep yours to yourselves, best that way. Now let's get your horses sorted.' He took us to the barn, brought out feed for Oliver and Finn and then led us back to the house.

'Are your sheep okay?' asked Tulip.

He opened the back door, it looked onto the yard and the sheep were milling about in it.

'They've not been harmed, just rounded up and loaded on that lorry.'

'Good,' I said.

'Thanks to you we got the word out in time. My sons blocked the two roads south and Fergus, from the next-door farm, blocked the west road. They were bottled up nice and sweet. When I got there, they were shouting at our Jack to let them through or they'd call the polis.'

'They've got a nerve!' I said.

The farmer nodded, a big smile on his face, 'aye and then the sergeant drove up with his constable, I said, you're just in time Sergeant Aird, these gentlemen want to make a complaint! The buggers blustered for a bit and then just gave up. They'd been caught red-handed. It was their own lorry too, so there wasn't much they could say. Been stealing for years. They'd been driving up from the South, grabbing a lorry load of sheep from the hills, keeping 'em a few months on their farm and then selling them on. They only have to do half the work, so they've been making a good profit.'

'That's so mean,' Tulip was shocked at such badness.

'Some people are like that,' the farmer said. 'At least these ones will be stuck in the nick for a few years. The sergeant says the bailie might make 'em sell their farm and maybe the farmers up here who've lost stock will get some money back.'

'Good!' I said.

The farmer's wife brought in a tray of coffee.

'I'd make them work on the farms too, make them do it and not get paid!' Tulip said firmly. 'They've been wicked and lazy, a few years shepherding in the hills would be a proper payback.'

'That's a good idea,' Morna said and put down a plate with squares of milk chocolate.

Tulip's eyes opened wide, 'CHOCOLATE!'

I pushed the plate towards her. 'I'm fine at the moment, you have what you want.'

'Where have you been staying …' the lady asked.

The farmer answered the question, 'been camping haven't you girls?'

I said 'yes', with a look to Tulip, 'we've been doing some

horse-packing. Gives us a chance to explore a bit further than usual and see new things. We live close to Edinburgh you see.'

'Found anything interesting,' the lady asked.

We told them about the places we'd discovered and the animals, birds and butterflies we'd seen.

'Lots of the animals aren't bothered by the horses so we can ride up and be sort of part of their world,' said Tulip.

We had a great chat and the farmer was very cool and made sure we didn't have to answer any difficult questions. When he had to go to work, we said we'd better get on too.

He took us back to the horses and asked us where we were going next.

'We're sort of on our way back now,' and I explained how we'd been doing a big circuit.

'Good on you girls. People should have a bit of adventure in their lives. I've been in the wilderness with … with a-a friend, he taught me how important it is to be able to deal to what's in front of you and you only find out what to do if you get out there and face it.'

We agreed.

'You've done us a good turn,' he said. 'There'll always be a safe place here if you need it … no questions asked.'

We said thank you, mounted and waved as we rode off.

Day 5
Chapter 3

'He knew!' said Tulip, once we were out of hearing.

'Whatever he knew it doesn't matter because if I come back, maybe he'll recognise me, but he's not going to remember you,' I said to reassure her.

'I wonder how …'

'He said himself, his family have been here for hundreds of years,' I reminded her.

'So?'

'And he said he's seen plenty.'

'How do you mean?' Tulip asked.

'I'd not thought about it before but … well … you can't be the only goblin … or even fairy, who's made friends with a human.'

She thought for a moment, calmed down and supposed that might be true.

'And the stories must have come from somewhere,' I pointed out, 'I mean I knew about pixies and fairies and goblins and trolls before I met you.'

'You didn't know the actual truth,' she said.

'I knew fairies were beautiful …'

'Beautiful airheads,' she conceded.

'And pixies were trouble makers …'

'Yes … but everyone knows that.'

I said humans must have had problems with them

otherwise how would we know.

'You didn't know goblins are the most wonderful, caring, beautiful, sensible people anywhere.'

'I do now … but that's because I've met Moo.'

'ME! That's how you know!' she claimed.

'Yeah, right.' I retorted. 'I tell you what I've learnt since I've met you Tulip, I've discovered Goblins can eat a wheelbarrow load of chocolate for their breakfast!'

She laughed, 'and I've learnt that humans can starve in a field full of vegetables.'

'Not me!'

'Only because I showed you …'

Well … I guess that was true so I changed the subject and said I had to teach her how to put her shorts on the right way or she'd have stuck them on her head!

'I would not!'

We let the horses amble up the trail and teased each other.

Eventually I asked her if they had any stories of goblins crossing over to our side.

'There aren't many,' she conceded. 'We've got lots of stories about how bad and cruel and mean humans are.'

'The stories could have been made up to frighten people so they wouldn't risk coming over.'

'That would make sense,' she agreed.

'Or I suppose … let's say years ago a goblin came across and they had just the most terrible time and wanted to warn everyone else.'

'Could have,' she said.

'We actually have lots of stories about fairies, some of them tell of how they come to help, some are about how they visit to steal our babies and others that they come to steal gold ...'

'They do like gold but why would they steal your babies?' she asked.

'Because they're jealous of how beautiful human babies are,' I explained.

'No, no way, NO! Human babies are ... well ... plain compared to fairy babies, it would be like a human looking at a cow parsley and saying "oooh, this must be the prettiest flower ever" and next to it there's an amazing rose!'

She had a point. Fairies are beautiful and their children are unbelievably lovely. 'Okay, I agree they're not going to steal our babies because they look so pretty, maybe they'd steal them because they're a lot cleverer than your average fairy.'

'That's definitely true,' said Tulip, 'but potatoes are cleverer than most fairies so it's not saying much.'

'Anyway, we do have plenty of tales even if we can't decide if fairies are good or bad.'

'I suppose if other goblins have come across and they became best friends with a human like I've done, they're probably not going to say to anyone back home. I mean I've been coming for years and still only Da and Moo know ... and it's not like I'm ever going to tell anyone else. For all I know every single goblin has been over and made a friend and they've all kept it a secret.'

I considered that for a moment. 'Do you know what I think, I think Ben the farmer did meet a goblin, he was looking at you a lot … as if you reminded him of someone. I mean otherwise why would he do that when I was standing right beside you?' I did a pose like a model, 'with my lovely blonde hair, my blue eyes and my amazing smile.'

'Blue eyes? Green eyes are better …' Tulip claimed.

'Maybe he couldn't believe what he was seeing, I mean coming face to face with a walking, talking poppy or perhaps he wondered why I'd brought a giant red crayon with me!'

'Red hair is the most beautiful,' she countered.

'I suppose red hair is okay … if you're a fox or a squirrel! Anyway, being serious he looked at you like he recognised you, like he'd seen someone like you before. And he knows about names, he knows how important they are. People over here usually don't know that sort of thing.'

'They don't do they? You know I thought I was the only Goblin to have made friends with a human but I suppose that's not likely is it?'

I agreed.

'There must be lots of kids like me who come over for a dare so why would I be the first to meet someone?'

'For sure … makes sense doesn't it?' I said. 'So maybe Farmer Ben met a goblin when he was a kid.'

'Could have done … but if it was a boy, they'd have only done stuff like kick footballs or dig holes …'

'Dig holes?'

'Yes, that's what boys do, or else they'd have played with

the tractors, because boys love toys, I bet they never went on wild adventures like we do; sailing the seas with pirates, saving la France from the Cardinal, going hunting with wild warriors and protecting the livestock from greedy raiders!'

'And they never had to worry about hungry wolf packs snapping at their heels, looking for a tasty dinner!' I said, I urged Finn into a canter so this time we were well ahead. She and Oliver chased us over the open moorland, past the hill fort and into a small valley.

We were back into the proper wild here. It didn't look like the farmers let their sheep come this far and there were no fences or walls. The horses were so much fitter so we went a long way before it was time to slow down. We stopped at a small stream slipped off and wandered along the bank. We found plenty of animal tracks and after studying them closely Tulip decided that rabbits, foxes, deer and goats were coming here to drink.

'Really?' I asked.

She crouched down next to the hoof marks and droppings and pointed out the differences. I was comparing the tracks when she gave a little shout, 'hey, look at these.'

She pointed to some more tracks.

'Those are cat prints,' I said, pleased I'd recognized them.

'Yes. A wild cat has been coming here too,' she agreed. 'They eat rabbits so he's after the bunnies.'

The horses were content being left to graze so we paddled in the stream and sat on a big flat stone in the middle to see if we could see if any of the wild life came out. We tried not to move or talk and it worked. Rabbits sidled out of the undergrowth, they weren't bothered about Oliver and Finn; although they didn't go too close. We'd hoped to see something a bit different but … well … it was just rabbits.

We'd been there for quite a while and I was about to stand up there was a rustle from the bushes.

A big, hairy, animal poked his head out, another pushed forward and then another, they had amazing corkscrew horns at least a foot long. It was the goats. They saw the horses and gave them a big "what are you doing HERE! This is OUR stream" glare. Oliver and Finn looked up, obviously didn't think the goats were anything to bother about and went back to munching quite unmoved. Since the glaring didn't work, the goats must have decided it was okay and edged forward, they were followed by the does and some very fluffy little kids. They gave Finn and Oliver a wide berth and went upstream twenty metres or so beyond us. They had a bit of a drink, a bit of a feed, the little ones played about and then they headed off. We let them get well away before we stood up, we didn't want to give them any reason not to come back here.

'What about that!' enthused Tulip.

'Brilliant! The babies are so cute,' I said.

It was time to get on, so we remounted and trotted along the side of the stream. A couple of grouse rose up out of the undergrowth, a rabbit hopped casually out of sight but the family of ducks didn't pay us any attention and continued paddling up and down feeding.

'They should be careful,' said Tulip.

'That wild cat or Mr Fox,' I suggested.

'Yeah.'

'The ducks will be safe in the water …' I said.

'I don't know … if he's hungry enough a Tod will go for a swim.'

'Really?'

'Uh-huh,' said Tulip. 'I mean it's not like they can't swim, they prefer to stay dry but you know a meal is a meal.'

Day 5
Chapter 4

We were well out in the boondocks now, and there was nothing to show that any other people had ever been here, there were no sheep or cattle and we couldn't see any traces of the modern world. Birds, hares, rabbits, mice, foxes, wild cats, insects and of course goats ruled the kingdoms here.

It was just wonderful.

I leant down, stroked Finn's ears and he gave a little neigh of pleasure. He and Oliver liked being on our expedition, the food was good, the water fresh and there were new things to see round every corner so they were relaxed and happy.

We trotted for miles and miles, marvelling at the emptiness, the ragged hills in the distance and the beautiful lochs in-between; everything stretched so far and the sky so big above us.

There was a big forest to our right and Tulip slowed down to have a better look.

'That's interesting,' she said.

It looked like just another wood and didn't look anything special to me.

'How do you mean?' I asked.

'It's really, really old.'

'Is it? How can you tell?'

'It's found a balance, the trees aren't competing they're happy where they are and with the tree next to them.'

As we got closer, I could see what she meant. The trees were settled, big old trees that looked like they'd been there forever and younger ones that might only be a few hundred years old.

'I don't think anyone's been in there for years and years,' she added, then something caught her eye.

'Hmmm …'

'What Tulip?'

'That's odd, there used to be a road going in to it.'

It was obvious once she'd pointed it out. There was a strip of grass a little browner than the grass on either side, slightly sunken and leading towards the forest.

'I wonder why,' I asked.

'A village is in there?' she suggested.

We trotted along the old path and up to the edge of the wood. Ivy was growing between the trees like a curtain and as Tulip rode up it moved aside for her to let us in. We rode through, the ivy closed up again and we were in a different world.

Although it was a mysterious forest it wasn't dark, spooky or scary. It was cooler under the trees but it was lovely, full of birdsong and everywhere butterflies and moths flitted about. There were plenty of fallen branches and dead leaves but the road was just about visible as it wound its way between the vast trunks.

'I think maybe the trees were planted on either side of the road,' said Tulip, 'it'd be a pretty big effort to put all this lot in just for a road between villages, so maybe there's something special down here a castle or even a palace!'

It was a long avenue so it took some time before we came to the edge, we left the shadow of the trees and found ourselves in a large, open meadow. An enormous bush was growing in the middle and we rode up to examine it.

As we got closer we could see it wasn't just one bush but lots of different climbing plants, all intertwined and growing over each other; wisteria, ivy, rambling roses, Virginia creeper, honeysuckle, vines, clematis and jasmine. Perfume from the flowers drifted over and it was just heavenly.

Tulip stared up at it for a long time, 'I think the plants have grown over a building,' she decided.

'There's a house under there? No way!'

'Uh-huh, come on, come on!'

We dismounted, Tulip raced off and I checked the meadow in case there was anything the horses shouldn't eat like foxgloves or ragwort. I had a good scout around and it was fine so I left them to ramble.

When I caught up with Tulip, she was underneath the flowers, breathing in the perfume.

I pulled at the grass and there was stone underneath, 'Hey you could be right these are steps.' I carefully moved the branches of one the bushes at the side and uncovered a bit of balustrade.

Tulip leant forward, the jasmine coiled around her and gave her a sort of welcome hug as if it was pleased she had come.

There wasn't an inch of brick or a single window visible

under the tangle of plants. If there was a house under it all, it was huge; as least as big as the one we'd visited when Dad took us to a vintage car rally last summer. Dad and Gus spent the afternoon in a muddy field going round the stalls and talking to people who had wonky tables full of rusty, broken bits of old motors to sell. Mum and I were NOT interested, we left them to it and went on a brilliant tour of the enormous, stately home next door. Afterwards we went to the tearoom, Mum bought us a fancy cream tea with cakes and sandwiches and then we watched a falconry display. It was incredible, the man just had to raise up his arm and the hawks and eagles did the most amazing things for him. When the show was over, we were allowed to go nearer; the birds were even more beautiful close up.

Tulip stayed where she was, with the jasmine wrapped around her and I thought she'd fallen asleep. She opened her eyes, 'come on,' she raced off to the back and I chased after her.

She stopped, started to climb and found what she was looking for.

'YES! Up here, Lorelei.'

She wriggled through a gap between the stems and disappeared.

I shinned up, twisted between the branches and found a tiny open window. I slipped through it and climbed down into a storeroom.

Day 5
Chapter 5

Tulip pulled open the door but before she could walk out I caught her arm.

'Hang on Tulip, we can't just go in, people are still living here,' I said in a whisper. 'Look!'

Instead of a messy ruin with bare walls and rotting floorboards ... everything was fresh, new and untouched. There were paintings on the walls, soft carpets on the floors and on the opposite side of the corridor was a big wooden dresser full of plates and cups.

'No, there's no one here,' Tulip insisted, stepped into the corridor and a little puff of dust rose up. 'And they've been gone for a long, long time,' she added.

I wasn't convinced, my nerves were on edge and I cautiously followed her down the corridor. She pushed open the first door, I held my breath and peeked in over her shoulder.

It was a large kitchen, there was no one there so we went in. And ... well Tulip was right, nobody was living here, it was all neat and tidy; except there was a thick layer of dust over everything; over the solid wooden table in the middle, over the pots and pans hanging above it, over the big metal dishes propped up on shelves around the walls, over the giant clay jars sat on the floor, over the huge, iron cooker, the skillet on the top and the bucket of wood logs at the side.

We went back out and carried on down to the entrance

hall. A big, solid front door was in the middle, above it was a double staircase and doors led off to rooms on all sides. It was like a palace, everything was made of white marble; the floor, the fireplace and the steps.

The drawing room doors were open and we went in. It was exquisite, loads of the sort of furniture the antiques shops sell but it was all new; elegant sofas, little tables beside them; soft carpets under foot; around the walls were cabinets full of silver teapots, jugs and cutlery, porcelain cups and saucers, in the gaps between the dressers were paintings and tapestries.

The plants growing over the windows must have protected everything inside from the sun so nothing was faded; the house looked like it must have done the day it was decorated.

'What happened here?' I wondered aloud.

'They didn't just leave,' said Tulip.

'How do you mean?'

'If they'd had to go in a hurry, they'd have left things lying about and it would have been untidy, wouldn't it?'

'I suppose,' I agreed.

'It's like they went on a trip and then never came back.'

'Super-weird!'

'I know,' she agreed.

We've been studying Jane Austen in class and the teacher showed us a film version of one her books. The heroine's house looked a lot like this place, so my guess is the last time people lived here must have been some two hundred years ago.

The first room at the top of the stairs was a massive bedroom, in the middle was a big double bed and curtains hung around it. Beside the window was a dressing table, on the top was a mirror with a fancy frame and lots of lovely things; perfume bottles, combs, clips, porcelain dishes and a dainty hairbrush with a silver handle. To the side was an open writing desk. I had a quick check in case there was a diary. There were lots of letters, a very soft piece of paper with ink marks all over it and a hard-backed book. It was a novel and someone had written in the margins, the handwriting was difficult to read but it wasn't like a journal, they were just making notes about the story and they'd underlined parts of the text like they were getting ready for an exam.

The plants were in the way so I couldn't see out the window so Tulip leant against it and they moved out the way. Finn and Oliver were calmly standing in the middle of the lawn looking quite content. Finn had a long bit of grass sticking out of his mouth, which made it look like he was chilling and waiting for his photo to be taken.

In a little room off to the side was a table with a china bowl, a big china jug and a carefully folded towel.

We wandered round the rest of the house. It looked like Tulip was right and the people who had lived here had gone on a trip. The chests of drawers still had things in them, the wardrobes were full of pretty dresses and old-fashioned suits. There were gaps here and there, so they'd taken some outfits but just the ones they'd needed for wherever they'd gone to.

In the children's rooms the toys, books and shoes were

all neatly in their places but some of the shelves had empty spaces as if there had been favourite treasures that just couldn't be left behind.

I suppose we could have stayed the night, the beds were even made, but somehow visiting and looking around seemed okay, but actually staying felt like we'd be trespassing.

'We shouldn't ever come back,' I said to Tulip. 'You know in case someone sees us and finds this house. I bet if they did, they'd want to take the paintings, the silver and the furniture or do something to the place or I guess live here.'

'It shouldn't be disturbed,' she agreed. 'I can feel a connection between the plants growing over the outside and the people who used to live here.'

'Do you think that's why the plants haven't grown into the house anywhere?'

Tulip nodded.

'Okay, when we get home, I'll speak to Isabella,' I decided. Isabella is my gran's special friend … this is another super weird thing, possibly even weirder than me having a goblin for a best mate. Isabella is an actual real witch and she's got properly powerful magic.

'That would be best,' agreed Tulip.

'She'll be able to come up with a spell to protect it.'

'You know when I first met her, I was really scared,' Tulip admitted, 'because … you know I could feel what she could do.'

'But when you get to know her, she's lovely,' I said.

Tulip agreed. 'So, if we're never coming back, we'd better

remember what it's like,' she suggested.

'Yeah!' I tried to fix in my mind, not what it exactly looked like but how it felt. It was so peaceful and everything in it seemed just perfect.

'You know I love our house, but I could live here,' Tulip admitted as we wandered round looking at the portraits

'Me too, dibs on the big bedroom at the front …'

'No that's mine … I'm taller so I need the space.'

'You can have that extra high broom closet at the back, being so tall it'd be perfect for you because you'd never bang your head.'

'And you'll be fine in that attic room on the north side, I know it's tiny but you're so small you'd still be able to lie down,' she countered.

We stopped in front of a big painting of the family. The father and mother were standing at the back, in front were two girls and an older boy.

'The girls are adorable … and the father is so handsome,' I said.

Tulip agreed, 'and the mum is simply perfect.'

'Look at them, so smart and well-dressed … I'd fit right in, I'd simply tie my hair back and there I'd be, sister number three, the sweetest, charmingest and most sensible one.' I sashayed around holding my hair in a ponytail, I nodded, curtsied and remarked about how charming Mama's new dress was. 'Of course Tulip, if you were going to put in an application to be number four YOU'D need a complete make-over!'

'No way, I'd be the precious, gifted one, who could wear what she wanted and become a famous painter.'

'Well you could start by painting the fence at home, dad was complaining it's getting tatty.'

'Artist then, like that lady!' she stuck her tongue out.

'All your paintings would be of chocolate,' I pointed out.

'I could paint them with chocolate, then the people who buy them would have something to lick if they were hungry after their tea,' she decided.

'You could make sculptures out of chocolate and that would be even better!' I recommended. 'Seriously though, it's really odd how the house has just been left. I sort of get the family might go off somewhere but what about the servants, I can't think they'd have all gone too? Even if they had, wouldn't they have left a caretaker or a someone to look after it? Okay, something bad might have happened to the family, I don't know what, maybe the ship they were on sank, or there was an earthquake but what about their relatives or the government people. Why didn't they come and do something? It's just been locked up.' I paused to think. 'And what about the postman … and usually these places have farms and horses and all that stuff. Where did the people who looked after the animals go? In fact, what about the animals?'

Tulip looked around and then gave a rueful smile, 'I don't know, Lori. You're right it is the strangest thing.'

Before we left, we looked in the larder. There was nothing, no sacks or jars or boxes. There was a cellar too, it was so cold we shivered as we went down. Stacked in racks were bottles of wine and on the floor small, wooden barrels … I suppose full of beer.

'Some people pay a fortune for old bottles of wine. I bet they'd love this,' I said. 'I wonder if it's still worth drinking.'

Tulip wrinkled her nose. 'Dad let me take a sip out of his glass once – yuck.'

'Yeah, I've tried some too, mum let me have a taste of her red wine, I didn't like it, it was sort of bitter. Mum said it's an acquired taste, but she says that about anything Gus and I don't like.'

'It must be worth acquiring,' decided Tulip, 'because people drink gallons of the stuff!'

We went back to the sitting room for one final look at the big family portrait, said goodbye to them and "thank you" for letting us visit and left through the window. We shut it as much as we could and except for the faint marks of our feet in the dust you couldn't tell anybody had been in the house since the day the family left.

Day 5
Chapter 6

We walked round the rest of the building, Finn saw us as we came round the corner and trotted over. He nuzzled my bag, he'd remembered we had carrots. Tulip called to Oliver so as to be sure they knew one of them wasn't getting a special treat. He came up looking curious and stood in front of her.

We gave them each a carrot and then it was time to get on.

We made our way back through the trees the ivy let us out, grew back over the gap and the forest became its own little world again; a secret jewel hidden in the middle.

'We're in for rain this evening,' said Tulip tasting the air.

'Are we? We should crack on then. There's a big reservoir to get past but then it won't be too far before we reach one of our old dens.'

We let the horses walk for a bit to get warmed up, then trotted for a few miles to make up for the time we'd spent in the house. We alternated walking and trotting and after a couple of hours there was a sheen of water in the distance. In the valley below the reservoir, houses were dotted here and there and further down was the town, two church steeples and a few tall chimneys stuck out over the other buildings.

'We can stay in the hills, we don't need to go near the town,' I said.

'Your towns smell dirty and smoky, the air catches my throat,' Tulip complained.

'I guess if you lived here all the time, you'd get used to it, but I do notice if I've not visited for a while my eyes itch afterwards.'

'And there are always horrid black marks on our clothes afterwards.'

'I think it's from the car exhausts.'

We jumped a gate and found ourselves in a field of black and white dairy cows, they looked up briefly with their big soft eyes and then carried on grazing.

'Did you know cows can jump,' Tulip asked.

'No way!'

'Sure! I've seen them. People think they can't but they can. I mean the cows in this field couldn't jump the gate we just came over but they'd get over smaller fences if they thought the grass on the other side was better.'

'Really?'

'Uh-huh and a fit, strong steer looks pretty amazing when he's going for it.'

Mrs. Lindsay often puts Finn and Oliver in with the dairy cows so they're used to them and calmly walked through the middle. Horses are picky eaters while the cows will eat anything so sharing a field isn't any problem.

We jumped the next wall and in the next field sheep were grazing. These ones moved out of our way as we headed to the banks of the reservoir. Tulip said it was curious how the sheep were staying well away from the water.

'Maybe they like the grass better where they are,' I suggested.

We stopped at the dam wall, it was vast, a big, steep, sloping grass bank and beyond it the loch sparkled in the sun. We were about to leave when we heard a faint creak.

'What was that?' asked Tulip.

'Probably an underground stream or more likely an overflow, you know to let the water out if the reservoir gets too full ...' I gave it some more thought, 'course it could be a channel like at the mill, a channel and they're using water to drive a wheel to make electricity.'

'No,' said Tulip after listening more intently.

'No?'

'It doesn't sound right,' Tulip said.

'How do you mean?'

'It doesn't sound like water going through a pipe or even like a stream.'

I got off Finn, crouched down to see if I could hear it better and Tulip joined me.

'Listen,' she said, 'it's definitely not a stream and I'm sure the ground is moving.'

I put my hands flat on the ground and it just felt solid like normal. I lay down and listened ... nothing.

'It sounds fine to me.'

'What do you think Oliver?' Tulip asked.

The horses were edgy and pulled on the reins to tug us away.

'They don't like it here. Look at all the lush grass round us but the sheep are staying way over there,' Tulip added.

'I don't know.'

'The sheep know something's wrong and so do the horses,' she insisted.

'Okay, I agree Oliver and Finn aren't happy …'

'And there's that weird noise …'

'But I can't hear anything,' I said.

'Honestly Lori it's not loud but it's there, we should tell someone.'

Tulip is far more sensitive than me so I said okay. 'We'll go down the valley to those houses and speak to the people who live there.' I suggested. 'They'll know if it's normal or something to worry about.'

Day 5
Chapter 7

We stopped at the first house, left the horses at the gate and went down the path together. The garden was very neat, grass tightly mown and not a single weed in the sparsely planted flower beds.

I knocked on the door.

A man answered it, took one look at us and before we had a chance to explain why we were there he swore … really loudly.

'… and take your damn lucky white heather with you. Don't you think I can pick my own? The hills are full of the stuff …'

I was so shocked I couldn't think of anything to say.

'Heather?' asked a puzzled Tulip.

I tried to concentrate on why we were there 'we've just come down from …'

'GET OFF MY BLOODY LAND!'

'The reservoir there's a sort of …' I tried again.

'I told you leave, do I need to call the police,' he said coldly.

We weren't getting anywhere so I caught hold of Tulip's arm and dragged her away before she started on the man.

He watched us go back to Finn and Oliver and then slammed the door.

'What on earth is wrong with him?' asked Tulip.

'That thing about white heather, he must think we're

Romanies …'

'So?'

'He can't like them,' I explained.

'Why?'

'I don't know,' I said, '… and he probably doesn't know why either.'

'That's stupid. He's stupid.' Tulip yelled at the house, 'YOU'RE STUPID! YOU'RE AS STUPID AS A RED-LEGGED PARTRIDGE.'

'Yes, yes … but come on. Let's not waste any time on him.'

'I CURSE YOUR CARROTS, MAY THEY BE INFESTED WITH FLEA BEETLES!' she added.

'Nice curse,' I said.

'Thanks,' she said. 'He looks like the sort of man who'd grow carrots.'

There was no car in the drive of the next house but we rang the bell any way. No one answered so we carried on to a small white cottage. The garden was a lot nicer than the first two, brightly coloured flowers had been allowed to grow wild everywhere, vegetables were planted higgledy-piggledy in the middle of everything and it smelt lovely.

A young lady answered the door. She was wearing a soft, colourful dress, a big orange scarf over her head and she looked like a hippy, a bit more like us.

'Hello girls,' she had a sort of breathless way of speaking.

'Hi,' I said.

'Where have you two precious seeds blown in from?'

Tulip and I looked at each other.

'We've just come from ...' said Tulip.

The lady interrupted her, 'what an exotic species you are.'

'Am I,' Tulip retreated behind me, worried the lady had recognized her.

I tried to get the conversation on track.

'We've just ridden down from the reservoir ...'

'Did the guardians speak to you?' she asked.

'Pardon?'

'They speak to me, they tell me their secrets and they help me choose which path is right for me.'

'Do they Miss ... do they?' This wasn't going quite how I'd expected. 'You hear voices up there?'

'Oh yes,' she said.

'We heard something too so we thought we should tell someone.'

'The spirits of the water are always helpful. Tell me dear what did they say?'

I stuttered to a halt, 'I-I-I ...'

'They were mumbling,' suggested Tulip, 'we didn't quite catch any actual words but they didn't sound like they were all that happy ... maybe they're ... er bothered?'

'Bothered? Oh I don't think so. You have to listen carefully,' the lady said, 'to really understand.'

'Maybe they need some attention, like from a reservoir doctor, perhaps you know someone you could tell,' said Tulip.

The lady looked like she didn't understand what we were on about so I decided we should cut our losses and try the next house.

'We'd better get on … say hello to the … the … er, guardians from us then,' I said and we left.

The next place was a modern bungalow with a stable to the side.

'Maybe someone who likes horses will be a bit more normal,' I said.

'Why? You like horses and you're far from normal,' said Tulip.

'I'm completely normal …'

At that moment a lady came out of the stable leading her horse. She waved to us and came over.

'Good afternoon girls, what a lovely stallion and the colt is already a fine animal.' She stroked Finn's flank. 'They're in tip-top condition, don't they look happy?'

'Yes miss, they've been getting a bit of a run out and been doing some exploring so I think they're pretty pleased with themselves …' I explained.

'Your mare is lovely too,' said Tulip.

The lady's horse leant forward to say hello to Finn and Oliver.

'This is Butterscotch, she's been a bit greedy recently so we're going to do some jumps. I think she knows she's in for a workout so she's being a bit standoffish.'

We explained that Oliver had been lazy recently but a week of riding had perked him up no end.

'Now he's keen to do the gallops, at first he just wanted to mooch around and eat,' said Tulip.

We chatted about the horses, she asked us if we lived near

and we told her how we were on a horse packing holiday.

'Good for you, a shame it's going to be wet this evening. Have you got somewhere to stay?'

We said we had and we probably best get on to it.

I remembered why we were there, so before we left, I said about the noises Tulip had heard.

The lady said she hadn't been up that way for a while. 'I can't think it's anything to worry about, girls. My best friend Faye, lives next door, she's very sensitive and says the spirits talk to her, but I think it's more likely to be something to do with the overflow; when the reservoir gets full the authorities run off some of the water. I'll say to my husband just to be sure. He's a geography teacher and he's always interested in things he can use in his lessons.'

Tulip said she felt something wasn't right. 'Miss, a few hours might not make a difference but I don't know … a day might, I think someone who knows should have a proper look,' she added.

'Don't worry, I'll ask Jack to check it out …'

'Are you sure,' I said. 'I mean if your husband is too busy, there might be someone else who could have a look?' I asked. 'If you say where they live, we could go and tell them.'

'Don't you worry and enjoy your holiday,' the lady said, then added that her husband would be back within the hour and she would make sure he went to check.

She insisted that we shouldn't put ourselves out. 'Jack will definitely go and check.'

'It's no trouble miss,' said Tulip.

'I tell you what,' the lady said. 'I've a friend who works in the council. I'll give him a call when Butterscotch and I get back from the jumps.'

That sounded okay and if her husband taught geography, it was the sort of thing he'd know about, so we said goodbye and set off.

That was the last house on the road, we looked down the valley and it was at least another mile to the next row of cottages.

'So ... do you think we should go down to those houses?' I wondered aloud.

'She seemed sensible ...' admitted Tulip.

'She promised to tell her husband, he's a teacher so he'll know about things like reservoirs ... and she said she'll phone her friend on the council ...'

'I don't want Finn and Oliver to get upset by the cars, lorries and people in the town but ...' said Tulip.

We hmm'ed and haw'ed but in the end decided the lady had promised us she would do something; anyway we couldn't knock on every door in the town and we didn't know if there was someone special we should tell and it was just a hunch. Tulip can feel illnesses but she admitted herself she didn't really know about things like the reservoir. We turned off the road as soon as we came to a farm trail. We'd been trotting for half a mile when we saw someone sorting out the hedgerow. He was weaving it so it was like a wicker fence and we stopped to say hello.

'Hello mister, this looks amazing,' Tulip gestured to the

finished hedge beyond him.

He stood up, stretched and said good afternoon.

'It looks so neat and tidy,' I said, '

He stared for a minute or so. 'I've not actually looked at what I've finished, hmm … it doesn't look too bad, I'm quite proud of that.'

'It's fantastic, can you show us how you do it?' Tulip asked.

'Sure Miss,' he said. He wasn't bothered by how we looked, how young we were or the horses looming over him.

He explained that the name for what he was doing was pleaching, he was cutting almost through a stem and then he could bend it and make a fence to stop the sheep or cows wandering. He let Tulip have a go. It took a few chops before she got the trunk cut right, then he directed how to twist it round and peg it in place.

He asked me if I'd like to try and I said 'that would be great.'

Tulip handed me the machete; the man indicated the angle and described the sort of cut I should be aiming for. I was a little tentative so it took me a couple more chops than Tulip but once it was done, I was able to bend the branch down and slot it round the stakes he'd already fitted.

'You don't sound like you come from round here,' I said, 'you must be really good if they bring you up here specially to do their hedges.'

'You're right, I'm not from here, I was born down south but I moved up for work about ten years ago.'

'It's great working outdoors all the time, isn't it?' said

Tulip, 'this is a perfect job.'

'Actually, it's more of a hobby …'

'A hobby?' I asked.

'Each year I try to learn something new, this year it's hedge-laying, last year I learnt to knit.'

'What a very cool plan,' decided Tulip.

'What's your real job?' I wondered.

'I'm an engineer, I work for a construction company.'

It would do no harm to ask him about the dam so I told him how we'd heard noises up at the reservoir and asked if I was right and the noises would be something to do with hydro power.

He looked curious, 'which reservoir?'

'The big one up there,' Tulip pointed to where we'd come from. 'I don't think it sounds right; I don't know, it feels like something is leaking where it shouldn't.'

'I didn't think they were generating power from that one. There's been talk about setting something up. In fact, I read some proposals a few months ago but since then I've been away for work and I had a few weeks holiday so I've not been keeping up to date.'

'I didn't hear anything except when we were ready to leave,' I admitted. 'There was a sort of creak, that's why I thought it might have been a turbine,'

The man rubbed his back. 'I could do with a bit of break after all the bending over. I'll go and have a look. I'd be interested to see if they've managed to get a generating system sorted.'

'Water power would be good, it'd be a lot better than burning coal,' I suggested.

'Indeed,' he agreed. 'The more renewable sources of energy the better.'

'We should get on,' Tulip said to me. 'It's going to rain this evening so we need to get sorted.'

We said goodbye to the man. He headed for his car and we got back on Finn and Oliver and set off at a trot.

Day 5
Chapter 8

We reached our camp just as it started to spit with rain. Last year we'd built a den here, so all we had to do was collect grass for our bedding and patch the holes in the roof.

We sorted out Finn and Oliver, checked them and made sure they were happy. We hung their food bags and the salt lick under a big beech near to the den, so they could feed and keep themselves dry overnight; not that they should be bothered by a bit of rain.

There were lots of edible plants about so we collected enough for dinner. We'd just finished as the rain started to get heavier. We crept into our shelter and sat in the door watching, at first it was just a drizzle and then a steady downpour.

'Funny how different all those people were,' said Tulip. 'That first man was totally angry and all we'd done is knock on his door.'

'I s'pose he could have been having a bad day. Perhaps he'd burnt his dinner, or his washing machine had blown up or he'd just found a hole in his roof …'

'I guess, but he didn't need to be so fierce,' she argued. 'Even if he had been having a bad day – well that was nothing to do with us. In fact, it might have been something we could have helped with if he'd asked. He should learn to be nicer to people.'

'Yeah, let's go back and burn his house down,' I said.

'LORELEI!' she slapped my hand, 'that would be going too far!'

I grinned.

'We could just burn down his toilet,' she giggled. 'Enough to be annoying but not enough to ruin his life. Why did he call white heather lucky?'

I said I hadn't a clue but I had heard people say it's a lucky charm.

'It's good for the bees and there are folk who say it's a medicine but Moo doesn't think it works,' Tulip said.

'I liked the lady in the cottage,' I said. 'Her garden was great.'

'And her water spirits?'

'There might be spirits, just because we didn't see them doesn't mean they don't exist. They might be like the pixies, we know when they're there even if no one else does.'

Tulip reluctantly agreed I had a point, 'although it's unlikely Lori. I think I'd know if a spirit was watching over the water.'

'You have special glasses?'

'Unlike you humans I'm not just super beautiful but I'm super sensitive too!'

The rain was forming big puddles in the little valley below our den, but at least it wasn't cold. Finn left the shelter of the tree, went out to take a drink and stood for a moment enjoying the feel of the rain on his back.

'Oliver is being all grown up again,' said Tulip.

He was watching Finn from beneath the tree and was obviously not planning on getting wet any time soon.

It was the last night of our trip and we stayed awake as long as we could, to enjoy the feeling of being outdoors. Much as I missed Mum, Dad and Gus, I liked having no clocks, no one planning things or wanting me to wear smart clothes and I really loved the times when it was just me and Tulip.

Day 6
Chapter 1

The next day the world smelt clean, the rain had perked up the plants and the countryside looked fresh. It must have rained most of the night because when we went to bed there had been a dry channel off to the side but now it was a noisy, tumbling stream and a decent enough pond had formed below us.

We washed our faces, checked Finn and Oliver and then found something for breakfast.

It looked like we were going to be lucky and the last day of our trip would be hot and sunny.

'This has been a brilliant week,' said Tulip as we gave the horses a brush down. 'I could go wandering with you forever.'

'It's been amazing that would be perfect.'

'I guess we'll have to get our own horses,' she said.

'Mrs. Lindsay would be a bit sad if we horse-napped Finn and Oliver.'

'Yes, stealing is very wrong. I suppose there'll be plenty of fun things to do when we get home.'

'Mrs. Lindsay's baby will be born soon, Mrs. Gardiner is picking up her new puppy next week and there're plenty of places around home we've never been to,' I pointed out.

'I know … it's just great being completely free. What have you thought of the trip Oliver?'

When he heard his name, he snorted and tossed his head.

Tulip went beside Oliver, she spoke in a deep voice and pretended it was Oliver speaking. "'I've had a great time, Tulip is the best rider ever, so much better than Lori.'"

'Finn begs to differ,' I countered.

"'Lorelei is like a bag of turnips when she's on my back, the big lumpy ones!'" Tulip added.

Finn gave a little whinny since we were paying more attention to Oliver.

'Finn says, "Tulip has no sense of direction. If she had been leading we'd have spent the week in dad's garage!"'

'We would not!'

'All oily and smelling of petrol just like dad!'

She reached up, grabbed a branch above us and shook it. A shower of water sprayed everywhere.

I managed to jump out the way so hardly any fell on me and most of it went over Tulip.

'WAH!' she screamed.

'Serves you right,' I laughed.

Finn shook himself and she got sprayed with even more cold water.

'Brrrr! I suppose I deserved that,' she admitted.

'Lori the sweetest, driest princess in the Kingdom,' I crowed, did a little twirl but lost my footing in the mud, slipped down the slope and landed on my bum in the big puddle at the bottom.

'EEEeeuhh!'

Tulip laughed, swaggered down to the edge looking well-pleased with herself and reached down to help me up, then before she knew it, I'd grabbed her hand, pulled her over and she landed in the puddle with a big splash. She sat there for a moment and then cupped some water and threw it over me.

I retaliated and in next to no time we were both soaking wet.

She stood up and waded through the pond pushing the water towards me with her hands.

There was a rustle from the other side, we froze and slowly turned to see who was making the noise.

A cow pushed through the bushes and stared at us with its big soulful eyes. It stayed there for maybe a minute, grunted and then walked on. Two calves quickly caught her up and followed her down the field.

It was time to get on. We squeezed out as much water as we could from our clothes, sorted out the camp, collected our things together and set off.

We walked beside Finn and Oliver until the sun came up, soon it was lovely and warm, the dampness in the air went and we dried off.

Day 6
Chapter 2

I'd deliberately chosen a roundabout route home as we hadn't properly explored this part of the countryside. At first, we made good progress but then the ground started to dip down steeply. There was a big river at the bottom, on the far side the water had carved out a cliff and above it was a tangle of brambles and hawthorns.

'There's no point in going down and trying to cross the river here. Even if it was just you and me, we'd find it hard enough to scramble up those cliffs let alone fight our way through that lot,' said Tulip, pointing to the bushes, 'and there's no way Oliver or Finn could climb up there.'

I agreed, 'yeah, they're horses not goats. That's a pain in the neck, I hadn't expected to find such a big valley here.'

There wasn't much else we could do, so we stayed on the ridge and followed the river downstream.

After ten minutes weaving between the trees Tulip spotted something, 'there's some sort of building over there.'

She's got pretty good eyes because we needed to get a lot closer before I could see what she was pointing to. Eventually I caught a glimpse of a large brick structure through the undergrowth.

'It looks like a bridge,' she decided.

'That's a bit of luck, it'll save us having to go all the way down the river … and if there's a bridge there should be a path or a road too,' I said.

The bushes and trees were all over the place, tangled and overgrown so if there was a path no one can have used it for months… well probably years as some of the trees were pretty big. We pushed our way round the trunks and through the bracken and shrubs and when we got to the bridge it didn't look like there was a trail on the other side either.

'This is weird,' I said.

'Why did they build such a big bridge but not build a road to or from it, what a waste of effort!' said Tulip.

It was massive and the people who'd designed it, had put a lot of work into making it look really good.

We dismounted to take a closer look.

It was paved down the middle, on either side was a three-foot-high parapet and at the foot wild strawberries were growing. The berries were tiny but sweet as anything. We ate them as we strolled along.

'Mmmm, these are "sooo" good,' I said

'We're lucky we got first dibs before the birds nabbed them,' said Tulip.

Half way across, I stopped and looked down. We were really high, below us the river wound through the valley and I spotted a heron.

'Look!' I pointed it out to Tulip.

He was standing like a statue in the middle. Suddenly he pecked down, caught a fish, swallowed it and then he was back to staring into the water.

Tulip was studying the structure, 'Lori, why is it such a

deep bridge?' she asked.

It was truly humungous; it must have been at least ten feet from where we were to the top of the arches holding it up. 'The arches are really big too, they look strong enough to carry a bus,' I agreed.

She stared along it. 'It's huge but there's no road on either side so no one is going to drive along here, so why?'

Tulip's riddle came back to me. 'Umm ... maybe it's carrying water,' I suggested, 'it could be a giant pipe to take the water from the reservoir we passed, to people in the city?'

Tulip lay down and listened. 'It could be a giant pipe, but I can't hear any water in it.'

'Maybe it's not being used today,' I said, 'maybe they're getting water from some other reservoir today so maybe they don't need to use this one right now.'

'Perhaps. It's not ruined or falling down, people are looking after it, the brick work looks good and solid and they've patched it up over there. How old is it?

'I don't know Tulip ... perhaps as old as our house, the bricks look a bit the same?'

'How old is your house, Lori?'

'Mum said it was built a hundred and fifty years ago.'

'So not very old?'

'How old is your house?'

'Hmmm, at least eight hundred years,' she decided.

'Your house does feel old,' I agreed, 'old and friendly.'

The bridge felt friendly too. Does that sound a bit mad? I mean it was just a bridge, people didn't live on it or anything, in fact we were probably the first people to go across it in ages. It just felt a good place to be, the strawberries, the warm red bricks and the river bustling along below us.

Finn wandered over to the far end and started sniffing at a bush, Oliver followed to see what he'd found.

'It's lovely here,' said Tulip. A dragonfly buzzed past. She held out her hand and it landed on her finger.

It was the most amazing colour, sort of silvery and also shiny blue green at the same time and its eyes were huge, almost the same size as its head.

It stayed for a minute and then it was away, the sun flashing off its body.

'I can't believe it actually landed on your hand!' I gasped.

'WOW!' agreed Tulip, 'I did not expect that. I'd only stuck my hand out as a joke, I never thought it'd settle!'

Two more appeared, I stuck my hand up high but they ignored me, kept on flying and were soon just a sparkle in the distance.

'Well, huh!' I said, pretending to be offended and we went across to Finn and Oliver to see what they'd found. It was a large bog-myrtle bush and even a few feet away the honey scent was strong.

'Do you like that smell, Finn,' asked Tulip.

Finn was breathing in deeply.

We didn't have anything that smelt of honey but Keir had given us some celery. He said Maeve liked it and it was good for her because it wasn't as sweet as a carrot but it was still crunchy.

Tulip offered them each a stalk. Oliver eyed his suspiciously. Finn didn't have any reservations, gently took it out of her hand and started chewing. Oliver doesn't like to be left out, he nudged her shoulder and she let him have his piece too.

They must have enjoyed it because as soon as they were finished, they nose-bumped us. We shared the rest between them and then had to show them the empty bag because they wanted more.

'Sorry boys,' I said, 'we'll have to wait until we get home now, that's it all gone.'

They pretended to sulk but we knew they were just playing.

There wasn't a path at the other end so we walked in front of them and pushed our way through the long grass and scrubby trees. The ground rose up gently at first and then started going down. We'd been walking in a straight line from the bridge and after half a mile we came across another strange building. It was a small, round tower with a domed roof, the windows were high up and they had metal grills over them.

'So, what's this?' asked Tulip.

We walked round, on the far side was a tough-looking, wooden door, I tugged it, but it was locked. We climbed on Oliver's back, as he's the taller, and looked through the grills but it was too dark inside to see anything.

I tapped the wall and then put my ear to it.

'Ah …' I said knowingly, 'well I never.'

'What, what is it?' she demanded.

'You'll never guess?'

'Tell, pleeease tell!'

'You can't say to anyone else!'

'I won't, I'm totally good at keeping secrets,' Tulip insisted.

'Well okay …' I looked around to check no one was listening in. 'It's a secret laboratory and this is their chimney.'

'Laboratory?'

'Yes, and down there are the most fantastical machines and they're using them to make the best tasting chocolate ever!'

'CHOCOLATE!'

'YES, YES! But …'

'But what?'

'It has to be kept a secret, otherwise hordes of people would be coming here demanding a share and as you can imagine chocolate makers need peace and quiet to make it best!'

'I could help them,' Tulip said.

'How,' I asked.

'I could taste it and tell them when it's perfect.'

'But you like ALL chocolate!' I pointed out. 'You'd be no good as a taster!'

'I would so!'

'They'd hand you the first piece and ask you to taste it, you'd go "ooh, yum, yum, yum". They'd make their notes then they'd hand you the second piece and you'd go "ooh, nom, nom, nom" and when they asked you which was the best instead of going this one is milkier or this one is sweeter or this one's too crunchy or this one's too chewy, you'd just go "they're both the best, can I have some more?"

'I would not!'

'You would.'

'Honestly, Lori, I'd carefully consider the milkiness, the sweetiness, the crunchiness and the chewiness… I'd even write it all down for them … and only then I'd ask for more.'

'Because you're so conscientious and because your writing is so neat, they'd be sure to give you the job.'

'And I'd be the best chocolate taster ever!' she insisted.

I thought some more about the building, 'you don't suppose this tower is something to do with the bridge, do you? The bricks and how it's built looks the same, don't you think, Tulip? TULIP!'

She was daydreaming about chocolate.

'What?'

'I was thinking the tower and the bridge look like they were built by the same people.'

'Yes, yes they do.'

Oliver was being very patient but he gave a little snort as if to say, come on let's get on.

'You're right Oliver, time to move,' I gave him a pat, slipped down, got back on Finn and we set off.

'Lori, if the bridge is really a big pipe to carry water do you think that tower was like a well and people would come here to get fresh water?'

I thought about that idea. 'Do you think people lived

round here.'

She had a quick look around. 'You're right, Lori-bobs, I don't think there was even a cottage let alone a village. Perhaps they used to come up here to let the sheep graze and it was easier to collect water from the tower rather than go all the way back to the farm?'

'Or if a big pipe is under here, maybe sometimes there's too much water in it and it needs an overflow, like in the bath?'

'It's a shame it's not working any more, after all the work the builders put in. Do you think nowadays they carry the water on lorries?'

That I was sure about. 'No, it's got to come through pipes, we all use so much of the stuff, baths, showers, loos and drinking, there'd never be enough lorries to carry it all. Dad might know or we can look it up on my computer when we get home.'

'It's not going to be anything as exciting as a chocolate factory but it would be a lot better if it was,' Tulip decided as we rode away.

Day 6
Chapter 3

When we were in the middle of our trip, we were properly in the wilds but now round nearly every corner was a farm or a house. It felt strange being back in civilisation, we passed hikers, farmers working in their fields and plenty of people with dogs, some of them had so many dogs they must have been walking them for other people. We got quite a few stares but we just smiled, said hello and rode on.

Three tough looking men were standing by a fence with their dogs. When they heard us, they turned and one of them opened his mouth. I was sure he was going to say something rude but Tulip gave Oliver a secret nudge, he jerked forward towards the men and they backed away and flattened themselves against the fence.

'OI!' one of them complained.

'Must have taken a fright when you moved,' Tulip claimed, pointing to the man wearing a camouflage top, 'he didn't see you there with your special jacket.'

'Oh … right!' the man said.

'You have to be real careful with horses,' she added. 'You know not shout or move too quickly, gets them right unsettled!'

The men obviously weren't happy around horses.

'You …' said one of the other men.

Oliver shook himself and pawed the ground.

'Quieter,' hissed Tulip, 'you've already made him edgy!'

The man looked properly nervous now and dropped his voice to a whisper. 'Sorry …'

'I can get him to do what I want when he's calm and not fretting,' she said, 'but he's big and if people shout …'

I had to force myself to look serious. I mean Oliver would do anything Tulip asked him to and he certainly wouldn't barge into the men just because they talked loudly.

'Aye he's a big bugger,' the first man whispered. 'We'll … er … let you get on.'

We deliberately got Finn and Oliver to walk off slowly and we heard the men breathing a sigh of relief once we were well away.

Day 6
Chapter 4

'I'm glad you didn't give those men a chance to be nasty,' I said.

'Good job they weren't used to horses,' Tulip replied. 'I don't know what's wrong with these people. Why do they think they can just say horrid things to strangers?'

'I bet they just don't think at all. They're with their mates, they're showing off and they probably think they're being clever or funny.'

'Well they're not! They're lucky I don't call Joseph on them!'

'My friends say they often get shouted at on the way to school when the boys are in their gang, but if there's one boy on his own, he'll slink about and try not to be noticed.'

We were still discussing the way boys act when we heard singing coming from the church on the other side of the river.

'That's lovely,' said Tulip.

'We've plenty of time, we're only a couple of hours away from home now, we could go a bit closer and we can hear them better,.'

The water wasn't deep so we didn't bother to go up the road to the bridge and rode across. We slipped off the horses and sat on a bench nearby. We'd been there for ten minutes when the minister came out, he saw us and came across.

'Good morning, ladies,' he said.

'Morning sir,' I replied and Tulip gave a little curtsey. 'Is it okay to listen?'

'Of course … you can come in, this is a rehearsal, the performance is tomorrow.'

'Are you sure … we're not really dressed for church …' I said.

'I don't mind,' he said and then gazed upwards, 'and god can see you out here and it plainly hasn't bothered him so far.'

Tulip looked up to see what he was looking at.

'… I can't think he'd mind if you came inside. Your horses are welcome to graze in the field, I'll open the gate.' He let Finn and Oliver in to the pasture next door and led us to the church.

'Been on an adventure?' he asked.

'Yes sir, we've been doing some exploring,' I agreed.

'And we've seen some amazing wildlife and found some plants I've never come across before,' added Tulip.

We chatted away until we were inside and then we stayed quiet so as not to disturb the singers.

It was lovely, it was just people singing, their voices echoing round the church. Tulip had never heard anything like it and was mesmerized. When the singing stopped, we clapped but not too loud because we were in church.

'That was totally thrilling,' she murmured. 'Wow!'

I whispered back, 'I'm in a choir at school and we sound like this … but of course much better because I'm singing with them!'

'How would the noise of an old creaky door improve anything, let alone something so wonderful?' she retorted.

'When we need a singer who sounds like a frog chatting to its mates we'll give you a call!' I murmured back.

'A frog who keeps in time, rather than a rickety gate that interrupts whenever there's a gust of wind …'

The choirmaster came over and asked if we'd enjoyed the performance.

We nodded.

'And do you sing ladies?'

'We were just discussing that,' I said.

'I sing like a bird but my friend sounds like an old door hinge that needs oiling,' offered Tulip.

'A goose is a bird and that's her singing!' I countered.

The lady smiled. 'Tomorrow we're doing some workshops and if you've got a little time, it would give two of our new teachers a chance to practice their lessons.'

'We can't stay long but we do have half an hour,' I said.

We each had our own coach; they took us to one side and ran through the lessons they'd prepared. My teacher was nervous at first, I think it was her first time doing this but she got more confident when she saw I really liked to learn. At the end we joined in with the choir and sang one of the songs we'd heard earlier. When it finished, they said thank you for our help, said we sang beautifully and told us they were impressed how quickly we learned.

We said we loved it and thank you but we'd better get off

home now.

When we went out Oliver saw us, gave a whinny and came over to the fence.

'He's more in tune than you were,' I said to Tulip.

'Creeeeeak!' she replied.

Finn was focussed on something in the corner of the field so I sent Tulip over to collect him while I went to thank the Minister.

I told him how much we'd enjoyed ourselves and how beautiful it was. He said it was all coming together and explained there would be a show each night for the next three days if we wanted to hear the whole thing.

Day 6
Chapter 5

We were back in familiar woods and fields now. We spent lots of time wandering here and it was cool to be on home territory again.

Finn and Oliver must have recognized where they were because they had a spring in their steps. They were definitely fitter and they'd enjoyed their trip as much as we had.

As we trotted down the back road to the farm Tulip said it had been the best holiday ever. 'I don't want it to ever stop.'

'It's been the greatest,' I agreed, 'I wish it could go on forever too but we've got other stuff to look forward to, different things and it'll make us appreciate the time we've just had.'

'You're so grown up.'

'Thanks …'

'It wasn't a compliment.'

'I'll take it how I like.'

'Although I suppose it's true,' she admitted. 'If you always do the same thing, even a fun thing, it'll get boring in the end. Anyway, we've finished our books so we need to go home to get some new ones.'

At the farm drive, Finn and Oliver picked up the pace and trotted through the yard back towards their stables. I suggested it must be time for their favourite telly program, Tulip thought they'd ordered a pizza and wanted to be sure

they were there when it arrived.

Mrs. Lindsay was sitting at her back door enjoying the sun, she looked up at the sound of hooves and waved. We went straight over and the horses nuzzled her. She asked us about our holiday and it was like opening a flood gate. We both starting talking at once, telling her about everything we'd done and seen and where we'd been and who we'd met and how brilliant it'd been and how wonderful Finn and Oliver had behaved.

She managed to calm us down after five minutes and got us to speak in turn. It must have still been a bit of a barrage of words but I guess it was a bit easier and hopefully she managed to piece together a little of what we'd been doing.

We carried on telling her our adventures as we said hello to Sally and sorted the horses out, groomed, fed and settled them in the stables. Afterwards Mrs. Lindsay let us have a shower. I went first, I'd left some home clothes with her, I tidied my hair so mum would approve, put on shoes and then we sat in the sun and chatted while Tulip had her wash.

Once we were neat and clean, we said thank you to Oliver and Finn, said bye to Mrs. Lindsay and headed home.

Day 6
Chapter 6

'Did the girls enjoy their expedition, Becca?' Mr. Lindsay asked and started bustling about the kitchen to prepare dinner.

She rubbed her back and settled in the big chair. 'If I get any bigger I'm going to need a hoist to help me stand up.' She patted her baby bump. 'I'm exhausted just listening to them, they appear to have packed a month of adventures into a week. They were buzzing.'

'I looked in on Oliver and Finn on the way past, they're looking as healthy as I've ever seen them, and happy, like the trip has done them the world of good.'

'They're going to miss all the attention when the girls are back in school,' Becca suggested.

'So where did they get to?' he asked.

She explained as much of the route as she could remember. 'Sounds like they were out in the wilds for most of the time and only went near civilisation if they couldn't find a route around.'

'How far did they get?'

'They turned back at Fuadain Waters, you know the big reservoir by Dunseil ...'

'They got away from there just in time then!'

'What do you mean?'

'It was just on the radio, the Fuadain dam burst late

yesterday and took out most of the town.'

'The town? GOOD GOD!'

'By chance someone was at the dam for a walk, realised something was up …' he shook his head.

'Oh goodness,' Becca gasped.

'He managed to give the authorities a bit of time.'

'What a disaster, t-the people.'

'I don't think anyone was killed, I didn't hear the whole report but it'll be on the telly.' He turned it on and found the news channel.

The camera was panning over a scene of devastation, houses, trees and roads had been swept away and huge pools of water were everywhere.

A reporter was interviewing a small group.

'Can you tell us what happened?' he asked a very shaken-looking older man.

'W-w-what a nightmare!' he stammered. 'We're lucky to be here, lucky to be alive,'

'So how did you get away.'

'I was out in the back garden, checking on my … my carrots, when there was a hammering on the front door. I confess I was a bit angry - it was the second time I'd been disturbed. I opened the door to give them a proper earful but this time a man was standing there, he said he was an engineer and told me I had to leave the house right away …'

'He was very serious, gestured to the reservoir and said he was extremely concerned about the integrity of the dam wall,' a man in a tweed jacket explained.

'Yes, and he told us not to go down the valley but head into the hills,' a lady in jodhpurs added, 'we fetched the horse, put the dogs on their leads and headed up the Giant's A... er the Giant's Rump.'

'Did he say who he was ...' queried the reporter.

'He ...'

'We should have paid more attention to what that girl said, she tried to warn us,' the jodhpur lady said.

'I should have gone straight up instead of hanging around checking my phone and having a beer,' her husband agreed.

'Girl?' asked the reporter.

'Yes,' a lady in brightly coloured clothes, clutching a cat, agreed. 'A girl on a horse, she looked like ... well it sounds a bit mad but she looked like a fairy, beautiful but delicate and insubstantial, she came by yesterday after lunch and said there were strange noises up at Fuadain.'

The first man looked guilty, 'yes Elspeth is right, I-I-I thought they were travellers or gypsies and I told her to leave me alone ... I shouldn't have been rude, I should have at least listened to what she had to say.'

'We all should have paid her more attention,' agreed the lady in the riding kit and perhaps that would have given the water engineers a bit more time.'

Mr. Lindsay and his wife looked at each other.

'Lori and Tulip!' he gasped.

'Must be, they said they'd been to the reservoir, Tulip said it was making strange sounds and she'd thought something was wrong. They knocked on the doors of the nearest houses to say they'd heard funny noises and maybe someone should check, none of the residents seemed bothered; they were told it was fine and they shouldn't worry.' Mrs. Lindsay recalled. 'Tulip admitted she didn't push it because she'd never been to a reservoir before so it could have been perfectly normal. Lori said one lady promised to get her husband to take a look and that she had a friend on the council and she'd let her know. The householders assured them it was fine, they were worrying too much and said to the girls they could head off to their camp as there wasn't a problem.'

'They really should have listened to them and not fobbed them off, just because they're dressed differently doesn't mean they're talking nonsense,' said Mr. Lindsay.

'Especially those two, I know they're young but they're so sensible.'

They turned back to the television.

'We stopped half way up the slope,' said the lady in the hippy clothes. 'I suppose we expected something to happen immediately but nothing did. After a couple of hours, we decided it was a false alarm but we sat for a bit longer just in case.

The lady in the jodhpurs agreed, 'we'd been debating whether we should head back and had pretty much decided to go home when it started.'

Her husband described it as being like a silent film, 'a wall of water appeared ...'

The shaken man breathed in deeply, 'then there was a noise like a clap of thunder, I don't think I've ever been so scared! That man saved our lives and the lives of everyone in town.'

186

Day 6
Chapter 7

The camera switched to a second reporter. She was standing on a ridge and behind her was a scene of devastation. A big crowd of people were milling about and most of them looked shell-shocked. The reporter was speaking to the camera and pointing out the waterlogged landmarks, the church spires, two tall chimneys, the town hall and the railway hotel and then she turned to a man in overalls and a woolly hat.

'I have with me Dr Forbes, a construction engineer, and the man who in all probability saved the lives of the people in this town. Welcome, Dr Forbes can you tell what happened?'

'I still can't believe it, all this destruction, it's hard to process,' he admitted.

'You were hedge-laying on the other side of the valley?'

Mrs Lindsay said the girls had spoken to a man who was hedge-laying. 'Lori said they'd told him about the noises because he was an engineer.'

'Yes, yes …' the man agreed, 'I'd taken up pleaching as a hobby this year and I'd got permission to practice on the hedges over to the south. These … this … a girl … horses … a girl on a horse was suddenly there. She looked fourteen, fifteen at most, hair bleached by the sun and just so vivid and alive looking … almost otherworldly. Anyway she asked me all about what I was doing and I showed them and let her have a go. We were chatting and when I told her I was an engineer, she said they'd just come from the reservoir and she'd heard an odd noise. She asked what did I think it might be. I said it could be coming from the overflow, they often run off water from these big reservoirs. She said it didn't sound like that, it was something else, something wrong under the ground she said.'

'What made you believe her?'

'To be honest I didn't … but I was curious, there'd been talk of installing a hydro-electric generator for years and I thought maybe it had finally been built.'

'And what did you find Dr Forbes …'

'Well there obviously wasn't a new power station and at first it all seemed completely normal although I thought it odd the sheep were staying well away from the reservoir wall. I had some equipment in the car so I thought I would just check the girl's story.'

'What did you discover?'

'The readings were off the scale. I've been involved in construction sites in Indonesia, so earthquakes have to be taken into account when we're building there. The feedback from the equipment suggested something similar so I didn't hang around. I thought it would be best to try and get the area cleared and then it could be checked properly. If it was okay, no harm done, just a bit of disruption for the residents if it wasn't … well better safe than sorry.'

'And …'

As I was leaving, I heard a screech, the girl said she'd heard a creak but this was really loud and it spooked the hell out of me, I raced to the car, drove down the lane and hammered on the doors of all the houses I came to. I must have looked pretty mad and maybe that's why they did what I said. I told them to get out and go as high into the hills as they could and I asked them to phone family, friends and neighbours; basically just make sure anyone in the way got out of the valley in case something happened. I phoned 999, the police agreed to evacuate the town and said they'd contact the water board and then I drove as far up the slope as I could. It's a big stretch of water, I thought if the retaining wall of the dam failed that sort of volume of water would do a whole lot of damage … and I really wanted to be well above it.'

'I can imagine,' said the reporter.

'I'd been there a couple of hours, phoning any government department I thought might be able to investigate. Once I'd done all I could and was sitting on my own thinking it over, well the doubts began to grow. Maybe I was wrong, maybe I'd misread the readings and I started to prepare a grovelling apology to everyone whose day I'd disrupted.'

'But you were right.'

'Sadly.'

'What happened next?'

'I was staring towards the dam when I saw the ground shiver and then buckle, the next moment water was pouring down like a tidal wave and the sound reached me.'

'Sound?'

'… this massive crash like a bomb exploding. Within minutes the valley had turned into a river and as you can see everything in its path was ripped away.'

'You're a hero, if …'

'No … if that girl hadn't stopped and asked me about it, she didn't need to, she'd already said to people. She's the real hero of this and she deserves the praise, goodness knows who she is.'

Day 6
Chapter 8

'And who they are is going to stay a mystery!' Mrs. Lindsay replied to the question posed on the television. 'I wouldn't wish the sort of attention the media give on anyone.'

'I agree,' said her husband. 'They did what they thought was right and not for anything more.' He turned to face her, '… you're not surprised they're only mentioning one girl. I know for a fact that when Tulip is visiting, they're inseparable. What's that about Becca?'

Mrs. Lindsay looked away trying to avoid his eyes.

'So …'

'If I tell you, you can't ever say …'

'What would I say?'

There was a long silence.

He backtracked, 'okay, it's something important and I guess I don't need to know.' He changed the subject. 'When's our next appointment at the antenatal clinic. I've seen so many lambs and calves being born I didn't expect to enjoy people telling me what to expect and what to do in the first few months … but it's been fascinating, I'm just hoping there isn't an exam at the end because the notes I've been taking are pretty hit-or-miss!'

'I've not been keeping secrets; it's just … well I think the fewer people who know the safer it'll be for Tulip.'

'Safer …'

'Yes, she's not … I don't think she's human and I'm sure she comes from a different place … so I think it must be something to do with that.'

Mr. Lindsay smiled, 'you know I thought there was something unusual about her, right from that first day I saw her. When you're brought up round here you see things and hear stuff. My gran told me stories about pixies, fairies and goblins. I'd put money on her being a goblin, too smart to be a fairy.'

His wife breathed a sigh of relief.

He continued, 'it's obvious Tulip is different, she has a connection with nature that Lori, despite being the wildest child you're ever likely to meet, doesn't have; she's too sophisticated … no … maybe worldly is a better word.'

Mrs. Lindsay gave him a hug. 'I've never asked either of them anything but Lori couldn't help letting little snippets of information out and I put them all together. You're right about Tulip, she has an innocence about the things teenagers are usually concerned about and then there's that intense relationship with the natural world.'

'She knows more about plants and animals than I could learn in a lifetime,' her husband agreed. 'You can rely on me to never say to anyone else. But why didn't any of the people on the telly mention her?'

'I haven't a clue. If they ever say I'll tell you but I probably won't ask. It seems a bit too personal.'

Day 6
Chapter 9

Gus spotted us as we were climbing over the garden fence and shouted to mum and dad.

'THEY'RE BACK!' He rushed across the big lawn and gave us both a big hug.

'Did you miss us little monster?' I asked.

'No,' he claimed, 'well a little … but only because I've been having to do ALL the work.'

'You've been doing all the work?' asked Tulip. 'You're so amazing Gus.'

'Yeah I am,' he said looking pleased with himself.

'Lori has been such a lazy lizard while we were away so it's time she took over from you,' Tulip added.

'Yes,' I said, 'I've been sitting around for a week … just planning routes, building shelters, finding food, looking after the horses and … and making sure Tulip didn't get into too much trouble!'

Gus thought for a moment, 'you're right, looking after Tulip is a full-time job, so "SHE" should take over and do my work now she's back!' he decided.

Dad was the next to arrive. He was in his dirty overalls and covered in oil and grease. He opened his arms to give us a hug.

We both backed away.

'Dad you've been working on your cars, you can hug us

when you're all clean, we don't want you smudging oil over us,' I said.

'Surely it's not going to make any difference, you'll be filthy after a week away from a proper bathroom.'

'Well we're not,' I pointed out.

'They smell of shampoo and soap,' said Gus.

'Even when we're out on a big, wild expedition we know how to keep clean,' said Tulip.

'We had a shower at the farm,' I admitted.

'Did YOU miss us?' asked Gus.

'And who are you?' I asked 'are you the new gardener?'

He gave me a push, 'did you?'

'Of course,' said Tulip.

'We had no one to tidy up after us …' I added.

'I know,' he agreed blithely.

'Well we missed you,' said dad.

'MUM,' I shouted as she walked down the path.

'Lori,' she replied, 'what's all the excitement?'

'You know we've been away so don't pretend to be all cool.'

She grinned and gave us a big hug. 'Did you have a good time?'

'Brilliant …' I said.

'Totally …' agreed Tulip.

We went back to the house.

'Dad fetched us some shop-bought cakes,' mum said, '… safer than me trying to bake.'

'Chocolate cakes,' dad added.

'They're just the best!' said Tulip.

Since the weather was still great, we set up outside, Tulip and I helped collect the coffee and cake and dad fetched the chairs.

Gus climbed on my lap and we sat in the sunshine.

Since we'd told the story once, we were a bit calmer and managed not to gabble and talk over each other quite as much. We told them about everything, all the things we'd done, the places we'd seen. We said about the gas smell near Castleton and how we'd done our good deed and warned the people in houses nearby …

'They were all lovely and so friendly and one little girl rode Finn with me …' I said.

'They were all really nice …' agreed Tulip, 'except that hoity, self-important Mrs Grier. Nobody who lived there liked her, we didn't even talk to her and we didn't like her either.'

'We read all about that, you were there?' said Mum.

'Yeah,' I said, '… what do you mean read about it?'

'So, what was the explosion like, must have been pretty scary?' asked dad.

'Explosion?' Tulip and I blurted out together

'When the house blew up,' said mum, 'I hope you were well out of the way.'

'There wasn't any explosion, everyone got out and the gas men blocked the road so no could get up there,' said Tulip.

'But your friend, the "hoity" woman?' said Dad.

'That Mrs Grier was definitely not our sort of person,' I said.

'No?' said Dad.

'The snooty bisom tonked her horn, acted like she was the most important person in the world and acted all superior to everyone …' said Tulip

'We left because Finn and Oliver didn't like the car horn,' I explained, 'and anyway the gas people were there, they were getting organised and that looked as exciting as it was going to get.'

'Well, you missed a treat,' Dad explained, 'according to the papers she used an app on her phone, switched on her gas heating remotely and …'

'Blew up her own house,' mum concluded.

'NO WAY!'

'Indeed Lorelei … way,' said Dad.

'But Lori warned them, she said to be careful and not to do anything that would make a spark,' said Tulip.

'She really blew up her own house?' I couldn't believe it.

'You didn't see any of this?' said Mum.

'Uh-no. We smelt the gas, warned the people in the houses and then headed off, we assumed it was all sorted.'

Gus asked what we were talking about. 'Why would someone blow up their house? If they wanted to blow up something they could blow up my school!'

'They didn't mean to,' mum said.

'They weren't thinking,' added dad.

'And they're not going to blow up your school,' I said.

'I wish I'd seen it,' said Tulip.

Day 6
Chapter 10

At dinner mum asked if we'd managed to fit in any saving of the world when we were away.

'We warned those people about the gas leak, it's not as big as saving the world but maybe we stopped anyone from getting hurt,' I said. 'Does that count?'

'I was under the impression you were on an "adventure" so I assumed you would have at least have rescued some kidnapped scientists, captured a few foreign spies but most definitely beaten up plenty of sinister, scar-faced villains with your amazing Kung Fu moves.'

'WOAH! Lori is that what you were doing when you were away?' asked Gus.

'Mum was being facetious,' I said.

Tulip and Gus both asked what facetious meant.

I said mum was making a joke about the spy-boy books.

'We're girls, we're not spy-boys,' said Tulip.

I explained about the books we read to Gus at bedtime.

'We did rescue that lamb,' Tulip pointed out.

'And we stopped the thieves who were stealing the farmer's sheep,' I added.

'You've been noble and selfless, I'm very glad you saved the lamb, poor little thing, and very pleased you used your nonces and weren't sucked down into the marsh but you can't claim it was you who stopped the sheep rustlers you just told the farmer,' said mum.

Dad pointed out that being aware and doing the right thing was just as important.

'And heroic,' I added.

'Lori, I'm not trying to belittle what you did,' said Mum, 'just making the point you used the skills we know you have and you didn't find out you could do karate out of the blue or were suddenly so clever you could work out a fiendish puzzle the best scientists in the world had been struggling to solve.'

'You've got to work with what you've got,' I said.

The phone rang and mum went off to answer it.

'I think you're heroes,' said Dad.

'Thanks Dad, although Mum's right we didn't need to be brave or do anything heroic …' I admitted.

Mum came back with the phone. She had her serious face on, 'Lori, it's the police, they want to speak to you.' She handed me the phone.

'Miss Lori Römer?'

'Yes sir?'

It was the policeman I'd spoken to when I'd phoned about the boys being rude and frightening. He wanted me to describe what had happened, what they'd said and wanted to check how I was. I said I was okay and told him exactly what they'd said, I admitted it had been scary at the time but I supposed it could have been a lot worse.

He asked me to repeat some bits because he wanted to be sure he written it down properly. When he was finished, I asked what would happen next and if I'd have to go to their police station. 'I hope the boys just get a telling off and they promise not to talk to people like that again.'

'They've had a serious talking to, they've been told how serious it is and warned if it happens again things will be taken further,' said the policeman.

'Because it's not nice to talk to anyone like that,' I said.

He agreed, then he told me the full story of what had happened. The boys had been very stupid indeed. The big idiots had kicked over beehives, the bees got mega angry and stung them and that was why they'd looked like they were drunk or been taking drugs. He explained one of the boys had been so poorly he was taken to hospital

'Oh …'

'It's just as well you phoned when you did, you probably saved his life. His reaction to the stings was so extreme he had to be rushed into intensive care … and he's still there …'

I didn't know what to say.

'His parents want to thank you …'

'I-I-I don't need thanks … I didn't really do anything … it was the doctors who saved him.'

He said to think about it, 'speak to your mum and dad and I'll be in touch later.'

When I put the phone down Mum instantly wanted to know why the police had phoned. 'What have you been doing Lori, why did they call and who did you save?'

'They wanted to thank us for capturing some awful spies, also for rescuing the prime minister and also for saving the world! He said we were heroes!'

'You didn't capture any spies,' interrupted Gus, 'you're not a spy-boy!'

Tulip ruffled his hair. 'We're spy-girls and we do even more exciting things than spy-boys,' she claimed.

'The truth Lori Römer,' demanded Mum.

'Okay. When we stopped at one of the towns to buy carrots for Finn and Oliver, three boys were hanging about outside the shop. They were really nasty, they said rude things about what they wanted to do to me ... you know grown up things.'

'You were really upset and scared,' said Tulip.

I leant against mum.

'I was but you cheered me up, Tulip. We left the village pretty quickly to avoid them. Then we saw them again and they were shouting and acting stupid.'

'We thought they had been drinking or maybe drugging,' added Tulip. 'We were super sensible, "WE" didn't even THINK to go and tell them off,' she threw me a look, 'instead "WE" decided Lori should phone the police.'

'Yes ... yes and I did, I said I was frightened.'

'Oh poor Lori ...' Mum gave me a hug.

'I'm okay now Mum.'

'Even from a distance they didn't look well, we thought maybe they needed a doctor or some medicine, so Lori told the police people about that too,' said Tulip.

'So why did the policeman phone, what did he want now?' mum asked.

'First he wanted to do his report so I had to tell him what

had happened, then he said, I put on a policeman type voice, "actually them boys weren't drunk, they'd kicked over beehives, the bees were raging, as you'd expect, and stung them and that's why they were acting stupid".'

'WHAT!' said Tulip

'I hate bees,' said Gus.

'Me too,' agreed Mum.

'He said one of the boys had an … annie-flactic …'

'Anaphylactic,' said Dad.

'Yes "anaphylactic reaction". The policeman said well done for phoning them, otherwise the boy might have … you know died.'

'I'm glad he didn't but what lummocks!' said Tulip.

'Just as well you did phone,' said Dad.

'Maybe you didn't rescue the prime minister,' said Mum, 'but what you did was even more heroic.'

'Maybe not heroic, but I'm relieved it wasn't as bad as it could have been.'

'So, you're not really a spy-girl,' complained Gus.

I tapped my nose, 'Gus, you really don't think I can just tell you, do you? You never know who might be listening?' I looked around as if checking for secret cameras. 'Top secret, don't you know!'

'You're not in trouble?' checked Dad.

'As if we would be,' I claimed.

'And is there anything else you've left out that you'd like to tell us before we get a phone call from the fire brigade or maybe even the army?' asked mum.

Two weeks later

Tulip was outside with Gus playing catch, mum and I were sitting in the kitchen chatting.

The radio was on and the announcer said, 'Welcome to "Front Row". Today we're lucky to have Martha Bailey, portrait painter and landscape artist, joining us. You have a new show, Martha.'

'Yes, I'm really looking forward to it …'

'And this is despite you've just come through quite a traumatic experience …'

It sounded interesting but at that moment Gus raced in. 'You've got to come, Tulip's found a dinosaur!'

'A dinosaur!' asked mum.

'Yeah, yeah come on, COME ON!' he ordered.

We left the radio playing to an empty room and rushed out to see the dinosaur.

'There, there …' Gus pointed excitedly.

It was a lizard, not quite the biggest one in the world but it looked lovely. It had a pattern of brown and yellow scales going in lines down its back. It was sitting on a rock. It didn't seem bothered about us and calmly lay sunning itself, occasionally flicking its tail.

'See! I think it's a baby stegosaurus or maybe a spinosaurus,' Gus explained. He had acquired a wide-ranging knowledge of dinosaurs even if hadn't learnt to shut doors, turn lights off … or flush the loo!

Mum asked Tulip what it was.

'It's a Gus-o-saurus …' she said nodding wisely to Gus. 'Or maybe a garden lizard.'

'Isn't he scared, shouldn't he be running away?' Mum wondered.

Tulip explained he'd just got up, 'he can't do too much yet, he has to sit in the sun and warm up before he can go about his business.'

'He's cold blooded you see,' I added.

'Can I have him?' asked Gus.

'I don't think that would be fair,' Mum said. 'He's a wild animal and he should be out here. Anyway, you don't know how to look after him or even what he eats and what if you get bored who would look after him then?'

'He could eat my vegetables …'

'He's not a veggie eater,' said Tulip, 'he prefers to eat flies, bugs and spiders.'

The lizard had warmed up enough and in a flash he was off.

'WOW! He's quick,' said Gus and went off in pursuit.

Dad shouted he was making coffee if anyone wanted some.

'We're coming,' I shouted back.

'Hot chocolate, please' called Tulip.

When we got back to the kitchen the radio presenter was saying goodbye to his guest and started playing her choice of music.

'This is a nice tune Dad,' I said.

'What?'

'On the radio.'

'I wasn't listening, just got a text from your granddad. He was at a car parts auction and managed to pick up some bits for the Wolseley project …'

Mum groaned. 'It doesn't need parts it needs scrapping.'

Dad ignored her disparaging remark and excitedly told us in great detail what it was Granddad had bought. He then started on a detailed explanation of what they would be used for.

It went over our heads, only Gus was interested and he wanted to go with dad and collect them right away.

Once we'd had our coffee Tulip and I went down to the farm so we could take Finn and Oliver out for a ride.

Autumn

Summer seems a long way away now. Tulip has been home for weeks and I'm getting to grips with the new school year. It's starting to get serious and next year I'll have to choose which subjects I'm going to stick with and which I'm going to drop.

We hardly saw dad for a couple of weeks as he was mucho busy, he had a trip to head office in London, he had to visit some of the local offices and then he was with one of his big clients for days. No sooner was he back but mum was away because she was speaking at an international conference. It was more relaxed with dad looking after us but there was a big down side. He couldn't cook … or shop … or make any decision about food buying; so we had three nights of fast food, a burger the first night, fried chicken the second and pizza the third. Gus thought he'd died and gone to heaven and I got a twenty-pound note to bribe me not to let on to mum.

On the Saturday dad announced we couldn't collect mum from the airport because he was expecting a delivery.

'You can't expect mum to get a taxi just because some rusty old car part is about to arrive, she'll kill you,' I warned him. 'Then she'll go to jail and my life will be ruined because I'll be the one stuck looking after "Monster boy"'.

'RRRRRAAARRGGH,' roared Gus.

'Calm down, precious flower …' Dad said pretending to

fan me.

'Dad I mean it! You'll be in so much trouble.'

'Breath in, centre yourself … actually it's a present for Mum. I bought it when I was in London the other week.'

'It's not Mum's birthday …'

'It's our wedding anniversary.'

'Oh … is it?' I asked.

'Yes. First time I've remembered,' he said, 'well second time, as I did remember the first one … after many, many increasingly unsubtle hints.'

'What have you got her then?'

'You'll have to wait and see sweet-pea.'

'Is it Lego?' asked Gus.

'Why would it be Lego, Gus-man?' I asked.

'Because that's the best present ever. I hope it's a space station!'

'A good guess, my best boy … but wrong, you'll have to try again,' said dad.

We kept guessing until the doorbell went.

I got to the door first. Two men were there and they had a large flat package between them.

'Mr Römer?' one of them asked.

'Yes,' I said.

'We was expecting you to be taller,' his mate said.

Dad came up behind me, 'this is my secretary, hired for her looks not her brains!'

'DAD!'

'So, is it Lego?' asked Gus.

Dad just rolled his eyes.

'It's a painting,' I said confidently.

'Yes,' agreed dad. 'Well done.'

I pointed to the van, the name "Fine Art Shippers" was painted on the side.

Dad signed the paper the man held out and they carried it in for us.

'Can we see it,' asked Gus.

'You'll have to wait for your mum, remember it's a present for her.'

'You're pretty chipper dad, you must be pretty confident she'll like it,' I suggested.

He just looked superior.

Mum's flight was delayed so we were able to pick her up anyway. We had lunch in the airport, she said it'd be a reward for leaving us with dad doing the cooking.

We didn't dare look at him in case we cracked, instead we said thank you and what a treat.

Gus had yet another burger and chips and I tried sushi for the first time. It was … okay … I had chips too.

When we got home, we had a grand unveiling.

Dad had struck gold; Mum was over the moon!

'It's amazing,' she said, 'I love it.'

I agreed with her, it really was amazing … although it looked weirdly familiar. It was a painting of a forest glade, in the middle, a girl was sitting on a horse and behind her was another horse and the way the bushes and trees were painted it could almost be as if someone was standing on its back.

'I was really taken with it because the rider looks a bit like Lorelei,' explained Dad.

'She does, doesn't she and the horse is lovely he could almost be Finn ...' agreed mum.

I studied the horse and mum was right, it looked an awful lot like Finn.

'Mum, Mum, come and see my Lego!' demanded Gus, he dragged her off to show her what he'd had been building while she was away and left me and dad with the painting.

'It really does look like me,' I said to Dad.

He agreed 'I know ... and the forest is exactly the sort of place you tell us you and Tulip camp out in.'

'Where did you find it?' I asked.

'When I was in London, I ran into Michael Yates and he invited me to a gallery opening. He's got a lot of connections with dealers, collectors and artists. He's friends with this lady, Martha Bailey, and introduced me.'

'She's really good.'

'It's fantastic isn't it? I had a good chat to her, she had a bit of scare a couple of months ago. She'd gone away to work on some of the paintings for the show and while she was there she had to be rushed into hospital with an aneurysm ...'

'Aneurysm?'

'It's like a heart attack but in the brain ...'

'Duh, I know what it is. Tulip and I got talking to a lady artist and Tulip sensed she needed a doctor because she had like a heart attack in her brain ... that would be super-spooky if it was the same person!'

'I've got the catalogue; her photo is in it.'

He fetched it from his study.

I couldn't believe it, it WAS the lady we'd met in the forest! I read the introduction at the front of the book, which explained how she'd been rushed to hospital in an ambulance, the doctors scanned her head and they were so worried she was taken straight into the operating room. According to the writer they'd put in a "stent" and caught the aneurysm before it burst. There was a paragraph from one of the doctors, who said she must be the luckiest person in the world because 'normally someone with an aneurysm only finds out after it has ruptured.'

There was a photo of the painting dad had brought and the notes said it was the first painting she'd done after they let her out of hospital. There was a bit the lady had written and it said exactly what had happened ... well except it only mentioned me, Finn and Oliver. The lady wrote that she'd met a wild looking girl doing some horse packing, they'd chatted, then out of the blue the girl told her she needed a doctor. Before she could stop her the girl had phoned 999. Miss Bailey said she'd been very annoyed at the time and only agreed to go because the girl seemed so convinced and had offered all the emergency money her parents had given her to the ambulance men to take her to be tested.

Dad was reading it over my shoulder. 'Is it the same person?' he asked.

'Definitely,' I said.

'There's no mention of Tulip. Just this mad looking blonde chick,' he pointed out.

'It doesn't say mad looking …'

'Where was Tulip?'

I made him promise never to say to anyone else, even Mum, and explained the weird thing about her name. 'But the trees at the back do look like there's someone standing on Oliver, don't they? It's like Miss Bailey knew someone else was there, even if she couldn't remember exactly what they looked like.'

Dad peered closely at the horse in the back. 'Those leaves could almost be wild red hair, couldn't they?'

'And the patchy sunlight could be her dinosaur shorts …'

'It was on sale for a fortune but the more I looked, the more I saw you in it and I had to have it. There was a 'for sale' sticker on it but the artist was very reluctant to let it go. She asked why I wanted it, she said it was little more than a sketch, insisted there were other paintings that were more valuable as part of her body of work but were on sale for less. I explained how I felt a connection to it and couldn't look at it without seeing my daughter. I added that sometimes you go away and then you're off for a whole month. I said I really missed you so if I had the painting it would be like you were still near me.

'She asked about you and I told her how you spend all your free time outside, that you ride and that the girl in the picture is as wild as you when your mum can't see you and she has blonde hair like yours …'

'But neater, let's not forget my hair is neater …'

He looked me up and down, 'yes of course, neater. Anyway, I asked her about it and she talked about her near-death experience and how the girl had probably saved her life. I said it was exactly the sort of thing you'd do. Of course, I thought she was living down south when all this had happened and she must have assumed that because I was at the opening I lived in London. The idea there might be a connection never crossed our minds. In the end she admitted the painting had been priced high because she hadn't wanted to sell but she was willing to let me have it as it seemed to mean so much to me, she even gave me a discount …'

'You must be pleased about that, Mr. Careful With-Money?'

'I would have offered her more to be honest Lorelei, I really wanted it.'

'Gosh …'

'Yes, and now I know it is actually you, well it makes it even more special.'

'We won't say to mum …' I suggested.

Dad agreed.

'My hair looks a bit too wild.'

'Artistic licence,' he proposed.

'But it is brilliant, it's exactly how it felt, the sun, the trees, everything green and fresh and I think she's even painted the squirrel nest we were looking at.'

Dad stared at it too, 'and you know, it takes me back to that time your Mum, Gus and I were stuck out in the wilds and you had to go and find help to rescue us.'

'Does it?'

'Just that feeling of being in the natural world,' he saw my expression. 'Yes, yes, I was terrified you wouldn't make it, I mean you were only eleven and there was nothing of you but at the same time the longer we were there, the more connected to the plants and the trees I felt. In the gallery this painting jumped out at me and instantly I could smell the pine trees and taste the wild raspberries we ate.'

'This is the first time you've been passionate about anything except cars,' I suggested.

'What are you implying Lorelei! I'm passionate about lots of things that aren't cars, your mother for starters, Gran and Granpa, Granny and Isabella, good food, wine, a fine malt whisky, our trips to Norway, old friends, the house, gadgets, my antique Parker fountain pen, boxsets, music, perfect spreadsheets, my old trainset, the clock your great-grandfather left me, you, Gus ...'

'How come we're so far down the list?'

He grinned. 'It's not ranked in any order, my sweet lily of the valley, it's simply a list.'

I gave him a stern look, 'yes Dad. Anyway I'm glad you bought this painting and I would have loved it even it wasn't me and Tulip who are the stars. Tulip will love it too and she'll be extra happy that she's sort of there but isn't really.'

Mum came back from admiring the boy's constructions and put her arm around Dad. 'This is truly the best present ever, I adore it. The girl does look a bit like Lori ... on a very bad hair day!'

Dad brushed an imaginary crumb off my top and made some "hilarious" comment about how I was such a neat little bobbin.

'And …' said Mum, she stared at the painting for a minute before continuing, 'you know the setting and everything reminds me of when we got stuck in that forest all those years ago and our little girl ran thirty miles to get help.'

'Like a spy girl,' I pointed out.

'Of course, like a spy girl!' She breathed in deeply, 'I can almost smell those pine trees.'

The End

214